THE NOT SO SIMPLE LIFE

Other books by Alayne Adams:

In Perfect Harmony

THE NOT SO SIMPLE LIFE

•

Alayne Adams

AVALON BOOKS
NEW YORK

All the characters in this book are fictitious,
and any resemblance to actual persons,
living or dead, is purely coincidental.
Published by Thomas Bouregy & Co., Inc.
160 Madison Avenue, New York, NY 10016

Library of Congress Cataloging-in-Publication Data

Adams, Alayne, 1970–
The not so simple life / Alayne Adams.
p. cm.
ISBN 978-0-8034-7753-7 (hardcover : acid-free paper)
I. Title.
PS3601.D3669N67 2010
813'.6—dc22
2009045268

PRINTED IN THE UNITED STATES OF AMERICA
ON ACID-FREE PAPER
BY HADDON CRAFTSMEN, BLOOMSBURG, PENNSYLVANIA

This book is dedicated to one of the most unique women I know: Kelly Kerstetter. For years you've amazed me with how you can go from 4-H Leader on the farm to Mary Kay Glam Girl to eCommerce Project Manager in the office. Your knowledge, energy, and sense of humor are marvelous gifts, and I adore you!

As with any endeavor of this size and scope, there are tons of people to thank, and my apologies to any I may forget to mention, but here's my best shot . . .

First and foremost, I thank my parents for allowing me to grow up in such a marvelous place as Nolensville, Tennessee, and its surrounding areas. Hopefully my "Cumberland Springs" stories will do justice to the places and people I know and love.

And the rest of my family—Eloise, Dud & Fran, Aunt Jean, Sheri & Ron (& Ryan), Jamie & Lizzy, Jason & Jami, and the adorable nephews and niece with whom to share my success, love, and laughter. Plus, the friends who are practically family—Michael & Claire, and the residents of Covington, Tennessee, who also hold a special place in my heart . . . and Jen M. who makes work fun.

I not only want to thank Kelly Kerstetter (4-H Leader), but also Melissa McDonald (Communications Director of the TN Board of Probation and Parole) for their help in research, as well as the staff and participants of the Perry County Fair (in PA), who welcomed me and spoke with me during the livestock judging events.

I'd also like to add a special thought and thank you to Ives, who helped me the day I did my last round of edits on the manuscript. *La vida no simple* has a much deeper meaning now. Your kindness and strength are unforgettable.

And then there's David Dippold, who makes sure every birthday is special and whose quiet dignity and fortitude is its own inspiration. You are in my head and my heart until the end of time.

Chapter One

Back when Cassidy French turned sixteen years old and started asking about things like boys and love, her grandmother had explained to her that love was just like the lottery: You never knew when your winning ticket would come around, but when it did, it would change your life forever.

So, it was safe to say that she had been warned when Mitchell Scott Riley accidentally stepped on her foot at Selby's Diner and ended up asking her on her very first date. He'd hypnotized her with those bright green eyes and that dimpled smile, and she'd been reeled in like a big old catfish in Percy Priest Lake.

Unfortunately, when Cassidy French turned nineteen years old, she also had to watch her father be taken away in handcuffs—handcuffs that her then-boyfriend Mitch Riley had placed on him.

She quickly forgot about love after that.

Of course, that had been almost ten years ago, and Cass had had plenty of things to divert her attention in the meantime. Her father's prison sentence, life on a family farm that showed little to no profit year after year, and her mother's surrender to cancer—life had ensured that she had no shortage of distractions.

Tonight, though, she found herself staring at the similarly charming eyes and smile of Mitch's younger sister Sally.

"Please, please, *please* let me, Cass. I know I can do it," Sally said. She pulled herself up to her full four-foot-ten-inches height and proclaimed, "It's what I was *born* to do."

The noises and smells of the Cumberland County Fair whirled around them as they walked away from the livestock pavilion. Laughter and applause skipped through Cass' ears just as the combined aromas of barbecued meats and simmering chili tickled her nose.

The sun had just gone down, and her stomach gave her a rumbling reminder that she hadn't eaten since she'd gotten here at noon. She zeroed in on the sweet, doughy smell of funnel cake and instinctively turned and stepped in the direction of the food vendors.

"I'm your Four-H leader, kiddo. It's not just my decision. We have to talk to your parents. I'd really feel better if you stuck with market hogs for another year or two before trying to move up to cattle."

"Age is just a state of mind. My grandma says so."

Cass smiled. Her own grandma said things like that too. "Look, your state of mind isn't gonna be worth a flip if a cow steps on you. It'll break your foot."

Sally rolled her eyes. "If one steps on *you*, it'll break your foot."

Cass didn't have a witty comeback for that one. What was it about Rileys and reason? They could get to her every time.

A series of delighted squeals erupted on their right, and Cass looked at the line to the ferris wheel.

Sally waved frantically to a car full of giggly girls. She cupped her hands and yelled, "Darla McIntyre, you were supposed to wait for me!"

The girls didn't seem to hear her, and she kicked the dirt. "Darn her. I wanted to go on the ferris wheel."

Cass glanced down at the matching yellow wristbands they'd been given as a perk of participating in the Four-H livestock competitions. The organizers always let the competing youth in free as an extra incentive to encourage their development of one of the most crucial factors in farming: successful raising of livestock.

"Tell you what. I'll go with you on the ferris wheel, and you have all the way around to convince me why I should let you change animal classes next year."

"Deal!" Sally said and bolted for the line to the ride.

Cass caught up to her in a couple of quick strides, and they joined the end of the line. They each had on their own version of their Four-H club's casual uniform, jeans and a green T-shirt with white lettering. An outline of a cloverleaf had been centered on the front of the shirt with each of the four H's represented on its own leaf. Head, heart, hands, health—the ingredients to form the whole person, the whole community.

Sally wore her thick brown hair in double French braids past her shoulder blades. If only she had freckles and lost that Riley dimple, she could have passed for Cass' twin back when Cass had been her age and a competitor.

Leaning and standing on tiptoe, Sally strained to get a look at the riders. "Look, it's Violet Simpson."

Cass glanced from car to car until she finally found the girl Sally referred to.

Shouts from another car quickly turned her attention.

"Hey, Sally Riley!" a male voice called from far above them.

"Sam Feldman, you stink!" Sally said then stuck her tongue out.

Cass followed Sally's attention just in time to see a

car teeming with boys, one of whom was mooning them.

"He'll be lucky if he doesn't fall and break his neck," Cass said.

She had no idea how he managed to maneuver himself out of the lap bar. She knew from the rumor mill, though, that when it came to mischief and Feldman boys, where there was a will, there was a way.

"He thinks he's so funny," Sally replied. "Let him try that down here on the ground, and I'll kick his butt."

Sally bounced with the energy that only the young had, and Cass felt an envious pang tug at her. Long ago, life had stolen that feeling from her, and she missed it. She'd love to feel the pure joy of running down the dirt road to the farmhouse, the wind in her hair, and nothing but the hum and energy of being alive coursing through her body.

Instead, when she drove down that dirt road now, all she could see was an aging property and a dying industry. Dollar signs covered the farm now, but they were red, not green, and she had no idea how to help.

Movement in the line pulled her back to the here and now, and eventually their turn came. The attendant motioned them toward a bright orange car. Sally slipped in first, then Cass moved in beside her. Some ferris wheels had gondola-like cages to carry the riders, but this one was more like a big metal bench with a rod that closed down over their laps.

The attendant locked them in and mumbled a list

of rules governing their riding experience. Sally turned and stretched, looking around at as many of the riders as she could.

She gasped. "Violet Simpson is alone in a car with Tommy Giles!"

"Should she not be?" Cass asked.

"She did the cake walk with Rodney Skinner today. Rodney and Tommy hate each other ever since football tryouts."

Sally gasped again. "And they're holding hands!"

She turned around and sat up straight. "Ooooh, there's gonna be a fight over this."

Cass did her best not to laugh out loud at the daily drama that was teenage life. The car moved forward two positions, and stopped, so the attendant could unload and load more riders.

"Aren't you supposed to be using this time to convince me of something?"

Sally changed topics on a dime. "Please let me do dairy cows next year. I know I can do it. Cattle are my life. I *love* cows. I wanna be the best dairy woman in all of Cumberland County. Heck, all of Tennessee!"

The ride moved again, gaining speed and going through several rotations. The cooling evening air rushed passed them, brushing Cass' face and through her hair. She closed her eyes and relished the prickle of the chill on her skin, the smells and sounds of the livestock and the food. These were the things that mattered. This was home.

Sally chattered on about everything she knew about dairy cows, and Cass smiled. Sally had such life and energy and talked on and on as though her body was filled with words that she had to get out or else she'd burst.

Such a difference from Mitch, she thought. Mitch was the stereotypical strong, silent, protective older brother—slow to speak and fast to act. He said what he meant and did what he said. And heaven help the person or thing that interfered with his family.

As Sally carried on, Cass realized that if it weren't for that endearing Riley dimple, she would have never even guessed they were related.

The ferris wheel slowed down, and Sally finally took a break from talking. Without warning, the ride suddenly made two loud screeches and stopped. The momentum rocked their car wildly, and Cass threw her right arm around Sally while grabbing the lap bar with her left hand.

Shrieks sounded from several of the cars.

"What was that?" Sally asked.

Cass held onto Sally until their car stopped rocking. "I have no idea. Seems like the ride just had some sort of problem."

"We better not be stuck up here long," Sally grumbled. "I have to meet someone."

"Oh?" Cass asked with a teasing lilt in her voice. "Is there someone out there *you'd* like to be holding hands with?"

"Yup. Carter Grayson," Sally answered without any hesitation, immune to the tease.

"I didn't realize you were sweet on him."

Sally crossed her arms. Cass let go of her, so she could settle back in the seat better.

"Oh yeah. I'm gonna marry that boy. With his family's corn, and my cattle, we'll have the best farm ever."

Cass smiled at the savvy little businesswoman beside her. "What about cute? Don't you think he's cute? It can't all be about business, you know."

A goofy grin lit up Sally's face. "Oh, he's hot." She gave a shy little shrug of her shoulders and leaned in closer to Cass before continuing. "I have a little secret. Last week, we were putting the balls away after gym class, and when we were in the closet, he kissed me."

"Really?"

"Yup. Good one too. That's when I knew I was gonna marry him instead of just thinking I might."

Cass chuckled.

"But I told him that if he ever told anyone what happened, or if he ever kissed me in public, I'd belt him one."

Cass laughed even harder.

Nonplussed, Sally stared up at her. "I mean it. I've got too many other things to do before I can get into all that kissing stuff."

"You don't exactly get to choose when you fall in love."

"I will. I've got it all figured out. First I'll finish high school, with all the grand champion titles I can earn, then we'll get married and settle on our own farm, just down the road from my folks."

Cass smiled. "I know you've heard me say this before. There's more to life than winning. So many things that you can't even *begin* to control go into the judges' decisions. The only thing you can do is focus on what you can control. Healthy, happy, hardy animals you're proud of—that's where your attention should be. Not on that trophy."

Sally didn't respond.

Cass ventured a glance over the side of the car and fought through a moment of queasiness as she did. They were only one position away from the very top of the ferris wheel, too high up for her comfort. She could see people gathering around the control booth, but she had to stop looking before the queasiness got worse. She checked her watch. Ten past eight.

The air whirled around them up here, and Sally shivered.

"We'll be warmer if we huddle," Cass said, curling her arm around the girl. Cass could feel waves of goosebumps breaking out all over her own bare arms.

"They better get a move on, or I'm gonna sic my brother on them."

"Aren't you a lucky girl? Not only do you have a big brother, but he's a sheriff's deputy too. You get double the protection."

"Yeah. It's pretty cool," Sally said, another shiver driving her closer to Cass.

The attendant came over the loudspeaker. "Attention, riders. We are currently experiencing technical difficulties. Please remain still and seated in your cars."

"Duh," Sally interjected. "What's he think we're gonna do, get out and swing around like monkeys?"

"Well, you never know about that Sam Feldman."

Sally laughed.

Half an hour later, they still hadn't budged. Cass couldn't help but notice that the neighboring sounds had died down, and the fair had become much more subdued. She glanced over the side once more. A large crowd had gathered below them, and, of course, every face was turned upward. Sirens wailed from every direction as all sorts of emergency vehicles finally arrived on the scene.

"This isn't funny anymore," Sally managed to say between chatters of her teeth.

"I know, but help is here now, so it can't be much longer."

She had barely finished her sentence when screams erupted from the ground below. Both she and Sally bent over the side and looked down. Cass could just make out the familiar form of Sam Feldman on the ground.

"Oh crap, oh crap, oh crap, Cass."

The car Sam had fallen from rocked wildly back and forth, jostling the other boy who had been with him. They were only about ten feet or so from the ground. Hopefully that was close enough for Sam not to be seriously hurt. The other boy wobbled, lost his footing, and flew over the front of the car. At the last second, his arm hooked over the lap bar, and he dangled from it.

Cass gasped, and Sally screamed, as did several onlookers.

"Don't look," Cass said, moving the arm she had around Sally and covering the girl's eyes with her hand. She had to clench her teeth together to keep them from chattering. At first she'd just been chilly, but now she was freezing, and she didn't have much pep left for a pep talk, especially with two boys' safety in such danger beneath them.

A voice boomed through the sheriff's car loudspeaker for everyone to clear the way, and the majority of the crowd parted as a cluster of firefighters scrambled to get a blanket beneath the boy.

Yet another voice echoed from below. This one was familiar.

"Attention, riders, this is the sheriff's department. Fire and rescue vehicles are here to begin evacuation procedures. Please remain calm and stay seated. Help is here. We're coming to help you."

"Mitch!" Sally called, tugging Cass' hands away

from her eyes and peering over the side. "Mitch is here. It's gonna be okay now."

Sally wrapped her arms around Cass and hugged her tightly. "I just want everything to be okay. Please let it be okay."

"It will be. We'll be fine now. Mitch is here. The other deputies are here. Fire trucks are here."

Cass held onto the shaking girl. She tilted her head, so she could look over the side, though. She could hear the boy's cries mixed with shouted commands among the rescue workers.

Two firefighters bent over Sam on the ground. They didn't move him but tended to him. Meanwhile a six-man team of firefighters and deputies scrambled beneath the other boy. She couldn't tell which one was Mitch. From up here, they looked like toy soldiers, and she couldn't make out any faces. They scurried and got the blanket spread between each rescuer.

A figure stepped forward. A deputy. Mitch. She could feel it.

He raised a bullhorn and addressed the boy. "This is Deputy Riley with the sheriff's department. We're going to help you. See all these rescue workers down here? They're here to help you. I'm going to count to three, then you can let go, and all these men are going to be here to catch you."

Cass watched as Mitch lowered the bullhorn and looked up at the boy, but she couldn't see any reaction from the child.

After a moment, he tipped his head back and yelled, "I want my mom. Please!"

Mitch raised the bullhorn once more. "We're going to get you to your mother, but you have to follow my instructions, okay? I'm going to count to three, and you let go. We're going to catch you. Then you can go see her, okay?"

He paused, but the boy said nothing else.

"Here we go. One . . . two . . . three."

The boy didn't let go.

"Listen up now. We're all here to help you. We're going to get you out of here. We're going to get you with your mom. Just let go on the count of three. You can do it. We're all right here, waiting for you."

"Did he do it yet? Did he let go?" Sally asked without moving from Cass' hug.

"Not yet, sweetie."

"I wish he'd hurry up and listen to Mitch."

The boy still swung side to side like a human pendulum. His arms slipped, then gave way, and he dropped. He cried out just as he caught the bar with his hands.

The crowd made a collective gasp, and so did Cass. Even with the blanket below him, there was a chance he might slip or fall at a wrong angle. The last thing Cass wanted to see was two boys' outlines on the ground.

Mitch called out to the boy again. "We've got you, son, just let go. All the men and women beneath you are looking right at you. They're right under you. Just let go. On the count of three this time. One . . . two . . . three . . . now!"

The boy finally let go and dropped right into the blanket. The team of rescuers closed in and lowered him to the ground.

Cass leaned back in her seat and breathed as slowly and deeply as she could. "It's all right now, Sally. It's okay. They got him down."

Sally pulled away and looked over the side. "Whew," she said with an exhale then leaned back in her seat. "What about Sam?" She peered over the side again.

"They haven't moved him yet. I can't tell anything more than that from here."

Cass took another look. "I don't think they fell terribly far. Hopefully we can find out more when we get down from here."

Sally shivered. Without the distraction of the rescue, the night air's chill crept right back upon Cass too. "You want to huddle up again?"

Sally scooted up against her, and Cass wrapped her right arm around her. "Don't worry. It won't be long now. Sure can feel the fall coming, huh?"

She gave Sally a little squeeze.

The car inched forward for several feet. Cass clutched the lap bar, and Sally tightened her hold on Cass. The car stopped.

Cass peered down to the workers below. A pair of rescuers helped two riders from their car. Another pair guided the riders to a triage station that had been set up at the back of a fire truck.

More rescuers stood off to the side. They held several ropes tied to one of the cars, and a line of volunteers pulled on the ropes. With a single shout, the helpers strained and pulled on the ropes, and the ferris wheel slowly turned again.

Another half hour passed, but it might as well have been half a day. Neither Cass nor Sally could control their shivers by the time they arrived at the bottom of the ferris wheel.

Once the lap bar was loosened, Cass helped Sally step over her and to safety first.

"Sally! I had no idea you were up there."

Mitch ran over and met her at the bottom of the ramp to the ride. He scooped her up and hugged her. He had his eyes closed, so he couldn't have seen Cass as she was helped out of the car.

"Are you hurt? Do you feel any pain anywhere?" a firefighter asked, forcing Cass' attention from Mitch. The fireman offered Cass a hand down the steps from the car and led her down the ramp.

She shook her head. "I'm fine. Better now that that ride's over."

He gave her a smile and attempted levity. "Seems like there are quite a few people here who should get their money back after this one."

"The little boy who fell? Do you know what happened to him?"

"Most likely a broken arm. They took him to County Hospital already."

They paused beside Mitch and Sally.

"You're shivering. Let's get you over to Mom and Dad," Mitch said, setting Sally down again. "They were over talking to the Simpsons, and they've got your jacket."

He took Sally's hand and took a step forward, but he stopped completely when he saw Cass.

"Cass? You were up there too?"

"She was with me. I was talking to her about Four-H stuff," Sally explained.

He turned Sally to the left and pointed. "Mom and Dad are over there. Go on, okay?"

Sally ran toward them, and Mitch turned back to Cass and the firefighter.

"I've got this one," he said.

The firefighter nodded and smiled at him. "Sure thing, Riley."

"Wow. Long time no talk. You okay?"

She shivered.

"Your lips are turning blue. Here." Mitch pulled off his deputy jacket, held it between his knees, then pulled off a navy-colored sweatshirt.

She reached for it then slipped it over her head. The heat from his body wrapped around her and seeped into her cool skin like the best hug she'd ever had.

"You all right?" he asked, pulling his jacket back on over the plain white tee he had on beneath the sweatshirt.

"No lasting damage," she said then smiled. "I'm just glad Sam's not hurt beyond a broken arm and that the other little boy got down okay."

"Well, I'm glad that you were there for Sally. I had no idea she was up there."

"We were having a bit of a sales meeting. She wants me to let her move up to dairy cows next year."

"Oh, Mom and Dad are gonna love that. I know it's normal for a lot of parents to fawn over their youngest, but they act like she's made of glass."

"I told her it was up to them."

She crossed her arms over her chest in a hug and soaked up even more of Mitch's heat. She already felt so much better.

And she could pick up the scent of his cologne now. Stetson. She'd forgotten just how good it smelled, just how good *he* always smelled. Dozens of memories and emotions rushed back to her.

"Wanna take a walk? I thought I might drive you home, if you'd like."

"Oh, I'll be all right."

"Well, just a walk to your car, then?"

She looked into those bright green eyes and felt the breath catch in her throat. Time away from him hadn't given her any immunity to them whatsoever.

"A walk to the car would be nice."

"Give me just a second."

He zipped up his jacket and walked over to another pair of deputies talking near the fire truck.

When she was sure he wasn't looking, she bowed her head and took in a deep whiff of his sweatshirt. Her nose was still cold, so she pulled the collar up a little and draped it on the end of her nose.

She looked over to where Sally had run to join her parents. The young girl leaned up against her mother who wrapped both arms around her. She chatted excitedly to them, no doubt playing spin doctor, so she could turn this trauma into her chance to upgrade to the animal class of her dreams.

Sally was no dummy.

Mitch returned to Cass. "Let's get you on your way to somewhere warmer."

They turned and walked toward the gate and parking lot closest to the livestock pavilion. He took a position beside her, not directly touching her, but not far enough away that she had to speak loudly at all.

"So how've you been?" Mitch asked. "Other than that new blue tinge, you look good, Cass."

She smiled. "You don't like me in blue?"

His face went blank, and she giggled.

"You're off the hook. I don't like me in *that* shade of blue, either."

His empty expression filled with relief.

"How'd Sally do today? I was on patrol earlier, so I couldn't make the judging."

"I'm sure she'll fill you in on all the details. The short answer is she made reserve."

"Second place isn't bad."

"Except that she's Little Miss Type A who wants to ace everything."

He shook his head. "Don't know where she gets that from. I wasn't like that."

"No, you always just wanted to be Mr. Average Joe. C's were fine. Lettering in a sport was good, but just playing was better."

"Sorta," he said with a hint of shyness.

As long as she had known him, he had never been able to see how he was anything *but* average, back then, and even more so now. When they had been teenagers, he had walked the halls of Cumberland Springs High School the same way he patrolled the county these days, like a modern-day warrior who never had to brag or even threaten. He just knew what was required to get the job done, then took the actions to do it. Emotions were never really part of the process.

Emotions were everything to her. So when he'd been there at her father's arrest, she couldn't help but lash out at him.

He was only doing his job. Her father had done wrong. Mitch was an officer of the law. It wasn't like he had framed her dad or even been the officer to make the case against him. He was just part of the team serving the warrant, a relatively safe errand for a new deputy.

She just happened to have been home when it happened, to have a front-row seat for it, just happened to hear the rapid clicks of the cuffs as they closed around his wrist. She could still hear those clicks, could still see that look on her dad's face, that wounded, ashamed look, and all she could do was stand there and cry. Those sounds, that look, her total helplessness—all of it had haunted her every day since.

"Which row?" Mitch asked as they reached the gravel parking lot.

She stopped walking. "Huh?"

"Where are you parked?"

"Sorry. Second row. Over there," she said and pointed toward her pickup.

They walked that way.

"You're allowed to be a little rattled. You were just trapped on the ferris wheel with my little sister, for how long?"

"*Too* long," Cass said with a smile. "Seriously, though, she's a great kid, and I adore her. I always have. She's like the little sister I never had."

Like the little sister I could've had, she thought.

The dimness that came over Mitch's eyes, together with his weighted pause, said the same thing, even though he didn't speak a word.

"Here we are," she said as they reached the pickup.

"Are you really okay?"

"So far, so good. I'm sure tomorrow will bring more of the same. It always seems to."

She stood at the driver-side door. Mitch took up a position next to the side mirror.

"I'm glad I got to talk to you, even if just for a little bit," he said softly. "I see you around town from time to time, but . . ." He shrugged. "Well, I never know if I should say something or not."

"Thanks for walking me to my car, Mitch. It was nice to talk to you too."

Cass pulled her keys out of her jeans' pocket and turned toward the door, then she turned back to him.

"Hey, you want your sweatshirt back?"

Her heart thudded rapid-fire in her chest. She didn't really want to give it back, but she'd rather not send him loaded signals, either.

He shook his head. "I've got a jacket. I'm all right. I'll get it some other time."

"Some other time, then," she said and climbed into the truck.

She rolled down the window. "Thanks again. Good night."

"G'night, Cassidy."

When she started the engine, Mitch stepped away. She rolled up the window, buckled her seat belt, then put the truck in gear and eased out of the parking space so as not to have the tires spit gravel at him.

She stole multiple glances at him in the rearview

mirror as she drove away and tried to get a grip on the mix of emotions that bombed her all at once. Her stomach lurched from the one-two punch of nerves and nausea.

Being close to Mitch was a whole bunch of things at the same time—familiar, comfortable, exciting. And then there was the painful element to it. He'd been part of the very night her family had fallen apart.

Forever would those things be linked. She already had enough trouble getting through the day without any new reminders of that night and all the horrible things that happened after it.

She mulled it over all the way home.

Chapter Two

Morning seemed to come earlier on a farm than most places, especially when that farm contained an overachieving rooster that prided itself in being ahead of even Mother Nature's schedule. He started crowing just as the sun had started to turn the sky grey.

Cecil, Cassidy's marmalade tomcat, voiced his protest with a half-meow as he rolled onto his back. Cassidy made a murmur of agreement and stretched her legs out. Cecil wrapped his front paws around her foot and rabbit-kicked her shin.

Cass yowled and sat up. "Hey, don't take it out on me. Go kick that rooster's fanny."

She slipped from beneath the covers as she had every day for years, now. She washed her face, brushed her teeth and hair, subdued the thick chestnut waves in a simple braid, then made her bed.

She dug the day's working clothes from the simple oak armoire that had been her mother's. Jeans, a navy tee, and a brown and gold flannel button-down shirt comprised today's wardrobe for the farm. Reluctant fingers pulled Mitch's sweatshirt off, but she put it to her face for one last whiff of Stetson before folding it and tucking it inside the bottom of the armoire.

She snagged the large basket by the door and headed down the stairs and toward the chicken coop. Unlike yesterday morning, though, she actually whistled.

After a quick stop to gather eggs, Cass walked into the kitchen. The usual smells of baking biscuits, sizzling sausage, and brewing coffee greeted her, punctuated by the sound of humming.

"Mornin', Nana," she said, stopping to kiss her grandmother on the cheek.

"Hello there, dear. How'd the judging go? Anything exciting happen?"

Cass set the basket of eggs on the kitchen counter. "Oh, my kids did fine. Nothing special beyond that, just got stuck on the ferris wheel for over an hour with one of the girls."

Cass grabbed a large bottle of apple juice from the fridge.

"You don't say," Nana replied in a tone that said she already knew what happened at the fair.

She lifted the splatter guard and flipped each of the sausage patties.

Cass opened the cabinet containing the glasses but stopped mid-reach and looked over her shoulder. "How do you do that? How did you already know?"

Her grandmother finished flipping the patties and replaced the guard. "So how is that Mitchell Riley doing? I heard you two were walking around the fair after he rescued you."

"Criminy, it's not even six-thirty in the morning, and you've had a play-by-play of something that happened after you were in bed last night."

"There are no secrets in a small town, dear."

"Yeah, who needs spycams or the Internet around here? The CIA could learn a thing or two from the data-gathering techniques of the sewing circles of Cumberland Springs, Tennessee."

Cass pulled three juice glasses out of the cabinet, then carried them, along with the juice, to the dining table. She set three complete places at the table while Nana put the finishing touches on breakfast.

Nana had just put the biscuits down on the table when the back door opened, and in walked her grandfather.

"How are my girls?" he asked, stomping and wiping his boots on the doormat.

His faithful, old, black-and-tan bloodhound Champ meandered in behind him.

Nana walked over and poured her husband a cup of coffee. She put two spoonsful of sugar in it then stirred it.

"Hey there, Pop Pop," Cass said, slipping into her chair.

"Mornin', hon," Nana said.

Pop Pop stopped in for a quick smooch with her before going over to the sink and washing his hands, and Champ took his place on an old horse blanket by the back door.

Pop Pop picked up the steaming cup of coffee, then took his place at the head of the table, but he waited for his wife to sit before he moved into his seat.

After a quick few words of grace, they dug into the feast.

"What's that you got there, Cassidy?" Pop Pop asked, reaching for her left ear. "Why, lookie there."

He pulled his hand back with a shiny quarter between his fingers.

Cass made the same well-practiced gasp that this morning ritual had allowed her to perfect over the years.

"You are amazing, Pop Pop."

"Me? You're the one with quarters growin' out your ears."

Nana buttered a biscuit and slipped it onto her husband's plate.

"Honestly, Hank, it's not like she's eight years old anymore."

"Oh, that's all right, Nana. If he keeps it up, I might

just be able to afford to go back to MTSU in a year or two."

"Schoolin', bah," Pop Pop grumbled as though the word alone threatened to ruin the meal. "School of hard knocks is the only college there is."

He carefully pushed aside several bites of egg and half a strip of bacon to one section of his plate then took his first forkful of egg for himself.

"If that's the case, then the three of us are all certified professors," Nana said, adding a little squeeze of honey over her grits.

They all busied themselves with digging into breakfast after that. Eating was serious business, especially the very first meal.

Cass waited until they'd all finished their meals before addressing the day ahead.

"If you don't need me after the morning chores, I have some Web pages to work on," she said.

"I've got both Dyer boys with me today, you just go on and do what you need to do."

Pop Pop stood, picking up his plate and coffee cup. He set the cup on the counter by the coffeemaker, then he carried his plate to where Champ lay and set it down beside his old friend. Champ sat up and immediately gobbled up the goodies his master had pushed aside for him at the beginning of the meal. Pop Pop poured his second cup of coffee.

"Who're you doing those page things for this time?" Nana asked.

"Marie Simon. She wants a customized, interactive Web site she can use for helping kids figure out college and financial aid. The government puts all these forms and things online, but they're about as clear as mud."

Nana perked up. "Oh my. Will she be coming by to pick them up? I'd better make a bundt cake."

"You don't pick up Web pages, Nana. There's nothing to pick up."

"How will she know you did the work, then?"

"Sounds like a pretty good racket to me," Pop Pop said then chuckled. "Modern-day snake oil salesmen."

"The pages are in the computer. I type a special code into the computer, then it creates the pages."

"Well, won't she want to come over and look at them on your computer, then?"

Cass shook her head. "It works like the TV or the radio. The computer sends the coded signal out to the rest of the world, and other computers out there know how to receive the signal and turn it into a picture that the person can look at."

"I declare. It all sounds so complicated. I can't believe you do all that from that little old space over the garage," Nana said and stood.

She gathered the silverware and her plate, then carried the pile to the sink. She rinsed them then placed them in the dishpan before moving to the stove to clear everything off of it. Pop Pop carried the now-empty plate from Champ to the sink and left it in the pan of suds.

Cass took her own dishes to the sink, concluding the ritual.

"You be sure to send those Dyer boys in after they finish the milking, Hank. They need a proper breakfast before they hit the fields today."

"Yes, Susan."

He drained the last of his coffee, walked over to the stove and gave her a peck on the cheek.

"Try not to spend all my money today," he added before walking out the back door.

Nana let out a heavy sigh. Cass knew all too well what that meant. *What money?*

"I'm having lunch with Beth today, so I'll see you around supper time."

"Beef stew tonight, sweetheart. Don't be late."

"Never in a million years."

She hugged her grandmother around the shoulders then took off for her garage apartment and a morning of heavy coding.

Fifteen minutes east of Cumberland Springs sat the Eversong Aviary, one of the real treasures of the county, if not the entire state. Ten acres of Tennessee hillside had been set aside and donated by the last heir of the Everson family.

The Eversons had been a dairy family who made a fortune during the mechanization of dairy milking.

The sole surviving heir had been the ever-reclusive nephew Trey.

Birds had been an obsession of his, and he'd taken a large chunk of his familial holdings and poured it into creating a fully endowed account to both create and ensure the long-term financial livelihood of an aviary and education center for his favorite creatures.

The place had proven to be a wildly successful field trip for every schoolkid from surrounding counties, often even further. College kids often came to intern from all over the country.

Cass pulled her pickup to a stop in the fire lane just outside the visitors' center. She dug her cell phone out of her jean pocket and dialed Beth.

"Bethany Fisher," her friend answered on a hissed exhale.

"Working hard?" Cass asked.

"Perfect timing. I'm ravenous. Are you out front?"

"Ready and waiting."

Beth often had a tight schedule at midday and didn't take a lunch at all when she had tour groups, but whenever her schedule was open, she insisted on lunching with her best bud.

She emerged from the main entrance and made a beeline for Cass' truck. She had on her usual green denim shorts and black Eversong Aviary staff polo shirt.

Once Beth was in and settled, Cass rolled out of the fire lane and drove toward town.

"So what's this I hear about you and Mitch seeing each other again?"

"Oh for Pete's sake! If people are going to gossip, they could at least get it right."

Beth snorted. "That defeats the whole purpose of gossip."

Cass stared out the window. "So do you want to hit Selby's or Tucker's?"

"Tucker's. Service is faster, and it's less likely we'll be overheard."

Cass glanced over at her friend. "What, do you know any good secrets?"

"No. You're just more likely to tell me all the juicy details if you think no one's listening."

Cass smirked.

"So did he kiss you?"

"Sheesh, Beth, all he did was walk me to the truck. He wasn't even the one who pulled me from the ferris wheel."

"What? What about the ferris wheel?"

Cass rolled her eyes. "I love how the gossipmongers probably told you exactly what I was wearing, exactly how close we were walking but failed to mention that the whole reason we even came in contact with one another last night was because the ferris wheel broke down, and a whole bunch of people got stuck on it."

"Aw, how romantic! Did he carry you to the ambulance?"

"I didn't need carrying."

"If I were you, I would've faked it. Have you seen the muscles that boy's put on since high school? Yum!"

"Have you forgotten he was there when my dad got arrested? He was part of the night my family fell apart. I said some *horrible* things to him after that. I told him I hated him, and that I never wanted to see him again. You don't go back to someone after that."

"Some folks do. Maybe he does." She cracked her window, letting the smell of fresh-cut grass fill the truck's cab.

"Maybe. Maybe not."

"Did he act like he was only doing his job? Did he act like he wanted to hurry up and get out of there?"

Cass went back over the evening in her head, although it didn't take a complete replay to get the answer.

"No."

She bit her lip and agonized over whether to let her friend in on the whole thing and let out some of the steam from the evening or whether to keep it to herself just a little bit longer.

"Oh, I know that look. You better 'fess up right now. He *did* kiss you, didn't he?"

"No, but he told me I look good."

Cass tried to exercise a little self-control and stop herself with one small revelation. If she told Beth about sleeping in Mitch's sweatshirt last night, the girl would start planning the wedding.

"And?"

Cass resisted the urge to let out an exasperated sigh. Beth would push for a complete reenactment if she thought she could get one.

"And he gave me his sweatshirt to wear because it turned so cold after the sun went down."

Beth made a series of short claps. "That's my boy!"

"He did something nice for me because I was freezing my fanny off. We are *not* getting back together."

"Cass, he's never gotten over you."

They pulled into Tucker's drive-in and rolled up to a parking spot on the far side of the restaurant.

While they ate the most delicious ooey, gooey cheeseburgers on the planet in the comfort and privacy of Cass' truck, Beth filled her in on how she knew Mitch had never gotten over Cass.

"He's only dated two other girls. Neither one lasted more than a month with him, and the rest of his time, he's either on patrol or working out." As an afterthought, she added, "Or with his family. That boy sure does love his family."

"There's nothing wrong with that. I love what's left of mine."

"Yeah, well, that's because you have the best grandparents in the world."

Cass smiled, although she felt a little sadness for her friend, who didn't have any grandparents left. Not only that, Beth had almost as sad a family history as her own.

Fisher men had big hearts, but they always seemed to give out on them. They died young. Beth lost both grandfathers before she'd even finished elementary school. And both grandmothers had been so overwhelmed with grief that each one had passed away within six months of their husbands.

They had only been thirteen when Beth's father had died in a tractor accident. Beth's mom immediately sold the farm and got off that "cursed land," as she called it.

The girls finished up their lunches and debated the dessert menu.

"I better get back, actually," Beth said. "We're having some reporter I have to babysit for a big part of the day tomorrow, so I have to make sure everything's in order today."

Cass started the engine and pulled out of their space. At the edge of Tucker's driveway, she paused for traffic to pass.

A white sheriff's car with green trim drove by, and Beth squealed.

"That's him!"

Beth waved, and Cass reached over to swat at her hand. Too late.

Mitch noticed them and tapped the brim of his hat at them.

Cass froze in place.

"Look at him. He's happy to see you. Come on. Live a little. You know you want to follow him."

"I thought you had to get back?"

"I might be willing to take one for the team, 'cuz if *you're* not due for some good fortune, I don't know who is."

"I'm not going to follow him in my truck. He knows my truck. And he just saw us staring at him."

Beth leaned back and put her feet up on the top of the dashboard.

"Spoilsport."

They teased and joked all the way back to the aviary.

Cass drove home, thankful for such a good friend and for something to do to keep her busy and distracted from the gorgeous, five-foot-ten-inch ghost with green eyes that had suddenly popped back into her life.

Between Four-H, her Web work, her chores for her grandparents, and her time with Beth, she could maintain the routine that had kept her busy enough not to notice the missing mother, the missing father, and the lack of a spouse or even a boyfriend.

But when she pulled into the driveway to the farm, she almost slammed on the brakes. A sheriff's patrol car sat beside the farmhouse.

By the car stood Pop Pop and Mitch, talking.

So much for the stay-busy-and-ignore-Mitch plan.

Chapter Three

Mitch looked so good, standing there in his uniform, right beside her grandfather. She couldn't pinpoint the exact emotion, but a warmth spread through her as she watched the two men interact.

But what was he doing there?

They turned and faced the truck as she pulled up next to the patrol car. She sucked in a quick breath before getting out.

"Well if it isn't the little lady herself," Pop Pop said as she approached the two men.

In the daylight, Cass could definitely make out the increased bulk and muscles Beth had mentioned at lunch. Mitch had always had muscles. He had played every sport in school, but maturity had added something extra special to them, to him. She had to force herself to stop staring.

"Hi, Pop Pop," she said as nonchalantly as she could. "Hello again, Mitch."

"Hey there, Cass."

"Guess I better get out there and check on those Dyer boys," Pop Pop said.

He reached out and shook Mitch's hand, clapping him on the upper arm a couple of times. "I expect you'll be runnin' for sheriff one of these days."

Mitch flashed him an "aw shucks" grin, and that dimple appeared. "I hadn't thought quite that far ahead, Mr. French."

"Well, you should. I know a few folks who'd vote for ya."

Cass' grandfather reached over and pinched her cheek as tenderly as his callused hands could.

"See you at supper," Cass said.

He winked at her then trudged off toward the barn.

Cass turned and met Mitch's gaze.

She almost lost the power of speech with those green eyes focused on her. She took a moment to study them. They didn't look fearful. They didn't seem angry.

"So," Mitch said.

"So," Cass replied.

"Wanna take a walk?"

"Is that why you stopped by? After all that sitting in your car, you need a walk?"

"Maybe," he said and adjusted his hat.

They fell into step beside one another. They crossed behind the house and into the side yard.

"What really brings you here?"

That "aw shucks" grin—and beloved dimple—appeared again, and he shrugged.

"I have no idea. I just wanted to. Thought I should check on you after your big, traumatic night."

She smiled. "I'm fine. How about Sally?"

"That kid? She bounced back as soon as Mom and Dad took her by the ice cream stand."

"She wanted ice cream after all that cold and shivering?"

He shrugged. "I don't try to understand her. I just try to live with her, or to stay out of her way when she's on a roll."

Cass grinned. "Good plan."

Their gazes lingered a little too long. She blinked first.

"What about the boys?"

"A bump or bruise here and there and one broken arm. All in all a minimal disaster."

"Glad to hear that."

Even though Cass felt true relief to hear that news, a tightness formed in her chest. An old and familiar burden returned. The nicer Mitch was toward her and the more he looked at her, the heavier it got.

"How are you, really, Cass? How's your dad?" he asked in a soft voice.

She looked away and into the distance.

"Me? I get by. Daddy gets by. He's a good man, a strong man. He never ran away from his responsibility. He makes the best use he can of his time. He teaches a *Bible* study."

She let the words trail off as the tightness in her chest spread up to her shoulders and hardened. *Just say the words. Get it off your chest.*

"This was never about whether he was a good man or not, Cass. I hope you know that. I know your dad's a good man. He didn't just teach me the Four-H stuff. He taught me just as much about life as my own father did. When I came here with the others that night . . ." He paused as his voice became choked with emotion.

She couldn't look at him, couldn't meet his gaze. Tears ballooned in her eyes, and she looked up at the sky, trying to will them to shrink back down and go away.

"I didn't sleep for days after that. I didn't sign on to arrest good men, men I respected as much as my old man. I almost quit."

She glanced at him then, and a tear rolled out of the corner of each eye.

The words came out at last. "I'm sorry, Mitch. I'm sorry for the things I said. Back then, I mean. I've never hated you a day in my life. Not even when it happened."

More tears came. Just as she was about to reach up

and wipe them away with the back of her hand he beat her to it.

He cupped the left side of her head in one hand and brushed the tears away with the back of his index finger.

"You think I don't know that?"

"I think." She sniffed. "I think I hate for you to see me this way."

Mitch shook his head and wiped away another of her tears with his thumb. He stroked her hair once, and she felt a tremendous urge not just to lean into the hand cupped at the side of her face, but to step forward and lean into a hug too.

"I've seen you a lot worse," he said. "I've seen you after a day of muckin' stalls. I've seen you," he said, pausing as some memory gave him a chuckle. "Remember the sheep judging at the Rutherford County Fair?"

Cass groaned. "Aw, not that."

They both chuckled at the memory of one rebellious little lamb that just would *not* line up with the others. Before the judge had even entered the ring, every other animal had taken a cue from hers and joined in a stampede that left her covered in sawdust that she needed three showers to get rid of.

They laughed for several moments. As the sweet sounds faded, Mitch's gaze met hers once more. This time, she didn't look away.

"I really am sorry," she said.

"Water under the bridge," he replied as he wiped a last tear from her left cheek. "C'mere."

He pulled her into a hug, and she melted into the embrace. The flesh-and-blood man surrounded her in even more warmth and comfort than his sweatshirt had.

She turned her face so that her cheek lay against his chest. She felt his chin touch the top of her head, and the reassuring weight settled against her.

His arms wrapped around her back, and she felt energized, cleansed, at peace. She closed her eyes and became acutely aware of everything around them.

The air was still, but she could smell wildflowers. She could hear the occasional lowing of cattle or neighing of horses. The steady, mechanical hum of farm equipment whirred in the background.

In the whole wide world, the only other time she got a feeling like this was when she sat down at Nana's table. A full table of food or not, Nana's table had a warmth and a comfort to it that banished all your worries, at least for a little while.

"Life really sucks sometimes, you know?" Cass asked as she thought about the series of events that had kept them from finishing what they'd started as teenagers.

"Yeah, but this isn't one of those times."

After several more moments of silent, healing hugs, they walked back to the farm house and to Mitch's cruiser.

"I'll see you soon, okay?" Mitched asked, standing beside the driver-side door.

"That'd be really nice."

He touched the brim of his hat at her, then climbed into his car and went back to making sure their little middle Tennessee county stayed safe.

Chapter Four

Cass had just finished creating the site map for Marie's new Web site and called to tell her that she could now test it, when her phone beeped at her that she had a text message. The number was Bethany's, and it was an emergency . . . of sorts.

9-1-1. Pick us up 4 lunch. Must see this reporter.

Cass texted back the three-letter code that meant she was on her way:

OMW.

She had just left the farm when Beth's next message arrived.

Go thru gift shop. Page us.

Cass made the drive along the back roads between her grandparents' farm and the aviary. If Beth wanted Cass to go through the official channels for visiting her pal, then that meant either she was trying to impress this guy or else someone important was watching. Cass guessed it was more the former than the latter.

What she couldn't figure out was why Beth would want her to meet some reporter, when her friend was rooting for a reunion with Mitch, anyway?

Maybe Beth wanted to go for him but just wanted Cass' opinion to seal the deal? The majority of men around town were boys they'd gone to school with, kids they'd known all their lives. Meeting a new guy, who was not only a looker but someone they didn't know as closely as any family member, ranked up there with walking out your front door and finding a brand new car in your driveway with the keys in the ignition.

Cass didn't really care what Beth might be trying to accomplish. Her mind kept going back to the yard and that tender embrace with Mitch. After all this time, she'd finally delivered the apology she owed him, and he'd been more than gracious about it. So much weight had been lifted off her, she needed the seat belt just to hold her down.

The biggest question left on her mind was whether

this apology was the ending punctuation mark to a long, drawn-out sentence, or was it the opening line in a new paragraph of their story?

She pulled into a parking spot in front of the visitors' center, and headed in through the gift store.

At the cash register stood a Cumberland Springs landmark: Immelda Watts. She had at least ten or more years on Nana. She'd taught Cass, her mother, and her father during their elementary years. She knew everything about everyone, and if you crossed her, she could curse your life in this town worse than if she'd been a full-blooded gypsy.

She had the white hair and rounded body that made her a perfect double for Mrs. Claus, but she had a sharp tongue that she could wield like a weapon if you set her off.

"Afternoon, Mrs. Watts. How are you?"

"I'm fat 'n' sassy 'n' proud of it. Cassidy French, c'mon over here and give your old teacher a hug."

Cass obeyed, and the women enjoyed a tight, jubilant embrace.

As they parted, Mrs. Watts said, "I declare, you look so much like your mamma did at your age, it's enough to fool this feeble old mind."

Cass blew a raspberry. "I want my mind to be 'feeble' like yours, some day."

"I suppose you're looking for Beth?"

"Sure am."

"I'll call her for you. Maybe that reporter fella is

still around too. Boy, he's quite a tall drink of water, if you don't mind my sayin'."

"I don't mind," Cass said then smiled.

Even though she'd been in this gift shop enough to know every knickknack forwards and backwards, she walked around the aisles of trinkets and goodies while Mrs. Watts called Bethany.

A few minutes later, Beth arrived. One look, and Cass knew exactly why Beth had not only called her over with a nine-one-one text but also insisted on the bigwig treatment.

A tall, slender man walked behind her with short but full jet-black hair and the most spectacular blue eyes Cass had ever seen.

Just looking into them was enough to send a shiver of delight straight down her spine, and she had to lick her lips to stir up some moisture because the rest of her mouth had suddenly gone dry.

"Cassidy French, I'd like to introduce you to a reporter from the *Cumberland Press*. Ty Thomas, this is Cassidy French, my best friend since kindergarten."

"Cassidy French? Why do I know that name?"

Cass and Beth looked at one another and shrugged.

"I thought we might take our guest to lunch in town," Beth said. "Selby's?"

"Fine by me," Cass said, pulling the truck keys out of her pocket.

This would be the other reason Beth called Cass to lunch. So she would drive, and so they would be in her truck where Beth would just *have* to sit up against the poor, unsuspecting guest.

"Lord help me, I'm gonna faint before the day is through," Beth whispered into Cass' ear as she settled into the middle space on the truck seat.

Ty climbed in beside Beth, and once everyone was settled, Cass drove them into town.

The lunchtime crowd had started to settle into Selby's, and they managed to grab the last booth before the worst of the crush. Naturally, Beth slipped into the booth, slid all the way to the wall, then patted the empty space beside her, and lured Ty her way.

"There's room here for you, Mr. Thomas."

He waited for Cass to take the place across from them, then he slipped in next to Beth.

All three of them turned their heads as a short, balding man in his fifties approached their table. He had on khaki slacks with a white button-down shirt and a red bow tie.

"Hello there, young ladies. Who's this stranger you've brought into my place?"

He looked directly at Ty and said, "I'm Gerald Selby."

He set down three glasses of iced tea in the middle of the table.

"You're on the tables today?" Beth asked.

"Yeah. Everyone's kids seem to have colds."

"Maybe they were all stuck on the ferris wheel in that chilly air?" Cass offered.

"And maybe pigs'll fly," Selby said, digging an order pad and pencil from the front of his white apron.

He leaned over to Cass and pretended to whisper but used his normal voice. "There's always some excuse when it comes to Miranda Carver."

Ty looked around the table then up at Selby. "Is there a menu?"

Selby laughed. "We got burgers, fries, and chicken. And on Fridays we have pork barbecue. Today's soup is corn chowder."

Ty gave a good-natured shrug. "Cholesterol, schmolesterol. I'll take a cheeseburger and fries."

Selby looked at Beth.

"I like that idea. Same for me."

Cass waited for Selby to finish writing then said, "Chicken sandwich for me, please."

Selby dropped three wrapped straws on the table then moved to the next table to greet more customers.

"So, how long have you been writing for the paper, Ty?"

"I've been a reporter since high school, really. The bug bit me when I wrote for my high school paper and just never let go. Got my journalism degree at Tennessee, and here I am. I've always liked the human interest angle to stories, so it's what I focus on now."

"Well, I can't wait to see what you have to say about us at Eversong. I'm sure it'll be fabulous."

Beth sure was laying the sugar on thick with Ty. If this kept up, Cass would have to ask Selby for a shot of insulin for dessert.

"Would you ladies excuse me?" Ty asked, standing up.

"Sure," they said in unison.

He took a quick look around, then walked toward the bathrooms.

Cass picked up her napkin, reached across the table and wiped the corner of Beth's mouth.

"You have a bit of drool there."

Beth fanned herself. "Isn't he something else?"

"Yeah, but you are trying *way* too hard."

"Am I?" She wrinkled up her nose. "I'm just so out of practice."

"You think *you're* out of practice? I haven't had a date since I was a teenager."

"Yeah, but the guy you're dating is already in love with you. It's an automatic home run."

"I'm not *dating* anyone right now."

Cass straightened. She hadn't had a chance to tell Beth about Mitch being at the farm when she drove back from lunch yesterday.

"What?" Beth asked.

Beth leaned forward and so did Cass, so she could fill her friend in with as quick a summary as she could fit in before Ty returned.

"Uh oh. This has the distinct look and feel of gossip," Ty said as he returned to his seat.

The girls broke apart. Cass glanced at him guiltily while Beth grabbed her tea and took a quick drink.

"So, Cassidy, what do you do?"

"I help out on my grandparents' farm, but I also build some Web pages for folks around town."

"All your family is here?"

"Well, it's just me and my grandparents."

Something flickered in those amazing blue eyes, something that disappeared before Cass could even begin to identify it. Before she could dwell on it, Selby arrived with their plates, and each one of them set about fixing up their food.

"So, do you think you're going to get everything you need in this visit?" Beth asked with a slightly more subdued eagerness as she spread mayonnaise on her bun.

"I don't see why not," Ty said.

He placed the slices of onions that came with the burger off to the side of his plate.

Cass carefully watched the looks going back and forth between Beth and Ty. He glanced at Beth, and his face changed, almost as if someone had just flipped a switch under the table.

"It's too soon to tell for sure, of course," he added.

Beth smiled at him.

In short order each of them turned full attention to the food. As a testament to how delicious their meals were, none of them said another word until every last bite was gone.

"Wow. Now that is one good, stick-to-your-ribs burger there," Ty said, wadding up his napkin and dropping it onto his plate.

"Isn't it?" Beth replied.

Cass pushed her plate back and settled deeper against the back of her seat. Very few things in the world felt as good as a full belly and good company, although she had yet to make a final decision about just how good of company Ty Thomas would prove to be.

She felt a prickle along her skin and looked up just in time to see Mitch walk through the door. Their eyes met, and everything and everyone in the room instantly seemed to stop.

Another deputy walked in behind him, bumping him in the back.

Cass stifled a laugh.

Beth and Ty turned around.

"Hi there, Mitch," Beth called, throwing a hand up in the air and giving him a big wave.

Cass kicked her foot.

"Ow!"

Beth turned around and glared at Cass, then she turned to Ty. "That's Mitchell Riley. He and Cass were high school sweethearts who never stopped bein' sweet on one another."

Ty looked over at Cass and winked at her. "So it's a man in uniform for you, huh?"

Cass picked up her glass of tea. "It's complicated," she said, then drained the remainder of the drink.

"You two ready to get back?" she asked.

"Don't you want to go say hello or something? Flirt a little?" Beth asked. She looked straight at Cass and mouthed the words "I do" to her.

Cass stood up and dug a few dollar bills out of her pocket, then dropped them on the table beside her plate.

"I thought you only get an hour for lunch," she said. "We should get going."

Ty and Beth exchanged glances. Cass left them at the table and walked up to the register.

"Heya, Selby. I need to settle up my part of the bill."

"Are you full and happy, Miss Cassidy?"

"You better believe it," she said, patting her stomach.

She gave him her money.

As he handed over the change, he said, "You give my best to your grandparents."

"Will do."

She should have walked straight out the door, but she couldn't stop herself from sneaking one last peek at Mitch.

He was chatting animatedly with the other deputy, and both men burst into laughter. As Mitch laughed, he glanced over at her. He winked, and she managed a small smile back.

She stepped outside with just a little extra pep in her step and waited for her passengers to join her.

After a quick drive to the outskirts of town, Cass rolled up to the curb.

"Thanks for the lift," Beth said. "I'll call you later."

Ty opened the truck door. "Nice to meet you," he said before getting out. He reached back to help Beth down, as well.

"Nice to meet you, too," Cass said.

Those brilliant blue eyes twinkled at her again, and she smiled before she could even think about it. He closed the door and took a step back.

Cass was just about to pull away when a sudden movement at the passenger window drew her attention.

Ty rapped on the glass, and she hit the switch to roll down the window.

"Your last name is French, did you say?"

Cass nodded.

"I just remembered where I know that name. Do you know anything about the man who killed his brother around here? I'm fairly certain his last name was French."

Inside and out, every inch of Cassidy turned to stone.

"That was my father," she said somberly.

"No kidding? I'd love to talk to you about that. What about his parents? Are they still in the area? I'd like to talk to them too."

"Nobody talks to them. They have no comment."

Ty studied her for a moment, and the stone inside of Cass morphed into solid steel.

"I don't mean to be insensitive. It's an incredible story, and I'm sure people would be fascinated by how you've all managed to cope with such a tragedy."

"There was an accident, and my uncle died. My father did *not* go out and intentionally kill his brother."

Cass leveled the iciest stare she could manage on him and did her best not to spit as she spoke, "If we wanted folks to know our business, Mr. Thomas, we'd live in a fishbowl in the middle of town, not on a farm on the outskirts of it. Good-bye."

She mashed the gas pedal and pulled away with a screech of the tires.

Chapter Five

"I can't believe how rude you were to Ty. Are you trying to ruin my chances or what?"

Thank goodness Cass and Beth were on the phone or else Beth would have been able to see Cass roll her eyes.

"It has nothing to do with you, Beth. You saw that greedy gleam in his eye the second he recognized my family's name. The only thing missing was the sound of a cash register bell as he realized he could get something out of meeting me."

"It wasn't *that* bad."

"Close enough."

"You're closer to me than my sister, so I'm going to say this. Has it crossed your mind that you might actually overreact to things like that sometimes?"

"No, it hasn't."

A wall of silence cropped up between them. There were a lot of things they could discuss, even debate, and their friendship never suffered any damage for it. Cass suddenly realized, however, that the trouble with her father didn't qualify as one of those things.

Of course, until today, they'd both been on the same side of the issue.

"If your hormones weren't raging, you'd see this more clearly."

"I'm going to go now," Beth said, and Cass could feel, just as much as hear, the sting in her voice. "Good-bye."

The display screen on the phone changed as Beth ended the call.

Cass stared at the numbers blinking and stating the call's duration. Two minutes and four seconds. That's all it had taken for them to hurt one another's feelings and undo decades of bonding?

Guilt nagged at her. Beth didn't know what it was like, having to protect people as innocent as her grandparents. They'd lost so much. They deserved as much peace and quiet as she could muster for them, and if that meant being a little rude to a reporter, then so be it.

She saved the HTML file she'd been editing and got up. Maybe a walk around the farm would help clear her head.

She headed out past the barn and into the lower

field where the cows were. She loved the sounds they made, the low hum of their calls to one another as they stood and surveyed the world while chewing on their cud.

They were all gathered together at the farthest end of the field and most of them were lying down. Cass knew what that meant.

Rain would be here soon.

A steady breeze blew from the west and had just a slight edge of a chill to it. Fall would definitely be here soon too.

The kids would have their last competitions in a couple of weeks, then they'd have the winter off, and they'd start right back up in March.

The tinkling of a bell interrupted Cass' thoughts, and she turned to see a very familiar cow headed her way.

"Hey, Molly," she called to the lumbering jersey cow. "You didn't have to get up."

She met her in a few strides, bent down and kissed Molly right in the middle of her broad forehead.

The cow let out a low murmur of approval. Cass closed the fingers of her right hand into a fist. She reached up under the tuft of hair at the top of Molly's forehead and dragged her knuckles back and forth across the fuzz-covered expanse.

The cow's eyelids closed halfway over the large brown eyes, and she made a series of loud smacking sounds with her mouth as she worked the cud.

Cass totally understood Sally's attraction to bovines. They gave off this aura of peace and understanding that could calm you even on your worst day.

In college Cass had made it through only one introductory class to religious studies, but she'd learned enough to know that cows were the Buddhists of the barnyard. They kept things simple. They had all the secrets of life cinched up: Eat, drink, stand around and meditate with your buddies, and if something irritates you, don't get worked up into a frenzy, use the minimal amount of force necessary—usually a swat of the tail—to dispense with it.

Molly had closed her eyes completely, and Cass slid her hand down the side of Molly's face. She brushed her fingers along the round, jutted bone of the cow's lower jaw and slowly rubbed back and forth.

Cass bent forward and pressed her forehead to Molly's. She breathed in the earthy, animally smell. An almost palpable wave of peace and relaxation rolled through their connection and worked its way throughout her body.

The worries that had been blocking her brain magically turned into puzzle pieces instead. The sensation was so realistic, she could practically feel them shift from immovable roadblocks into a cohesive picture.

She knew what she would do. She would apologize to Beth, even though she didn't feel fully to blame. Part of being a good friend, though, was knowing what to say and when. She and Beth had been at one another's side since kindergarten, and she wasn't going to let anything happen to that just because she'd shot her mouth off to a reporter who had rubbed her the wrong way.

Then she would find a way to ask Mitch out. The new millennium had come and gone, and a girl could ask a guy on a date without waiting for Sadie Hawkins Day.

But would he say yes? It was one thing to accept someone's long-overdue apology. It was another thing altogether to let that person back into your life.

No matter what the answer might be, the time had come to let just a little goodness in and see if she couldn't find a way to make it stay this time.

Cass slowly made her way back toward the farmhouse kitchen. She wiped her feet off, and she heard movement inside the kitchen.

"Is that you, Hank?" Nana called.

"It's me, Nana."

"Oh, good. You don't mind running these eggs into Selby's do you? He says he's a bit short this week and wanted to buy any extras we had."

"Not at all."

Cass walked to the refrigerator and pulled out a can of Mountain Dew. "I just need to make a couple of quick changes to Marie's site, then I'll head into town."

"You didn't eat much breakfast. I could fix you a nice lunch."

"That's okay. I'm not very hungry."

"Are you all right?"

"Just a lot on my mind, Nana."

"It'll be visitation day soon."

Cass paused. She hadn't thought about that, but Nana was right. It'd be visitation day at the end of the week, and she'd have to make the long drive to Nashville to Riverbend Prison.

Oh well, she'd deal with that later.

Nana probably blamed her distraction on that. Instead, Cass had the one-two punch of the run-ins with Mitch, plus, this reporter who could start poking around any day now.

No matter what, she would not let that happen. Her grandparents had already been through enough. They'd buried a child. They'd seen another go to jail for it. Then they'd had to help care for Mamma as cancer ravaged her body. Legal and medical costs obliterated their income and savings. They hung onto the farm by the skin of their teeth.

No stranger would intrude on what little peace and quiet they had left and put them back in the spotlight. Not as long as she had anything to say about it.

A couple of hours later, she dropped the eggs off at Selby's then crossed the street to Simon's Drugstore to see Marie and pick up her payment for the Web site. Doing these small, infrequent jobs, she didn't make the money she could have in a major city, but a lot of the businesses here were just figuring out the power of the Web and automating themselves.

If only she could figure out a way to put the Web to work for her grandparents, she just might be able to ease their burdens. Of course, she could outsource her services to bigger companies too. She just needed a chance to research the possibility.

"Cassidy French, what a surprise," a male voice called from behind her.

She whirled around and smiled in recognition of the man who had served as her father's lawyer.

"Norm Greer, how are you?"

She walked up and hugged the huge mountain of a man. Whoever invented the phrase "fat cat lawyer" probably had a man like Norm in mind. Outside of the courtroom, he was tame as any lap cat, but once the judge pounded that gavel, he fought tooth and nail for his clients. He had argued so hard for her father, he'd actually been found in contempt of court, fined, and put in jail for a night.

"I was just thinking about you," he said, giving her a hearty squeeze. "How about you let an old man buy you something to eat?"

"Aw, you don't have to do that."

"It'd be my pleasure. I wanted to talk to you about your father, anyway."

She followed him into Selby's Diner.

They slipped into a booth. Within moments, Selby delivered two iced teas.

"Back in a minute to take your orders," he said before taking off to another table.

"Is my dad okay?"

"He's fine. Actually, I just got the notice for his parole hearing in a few weeks, and I wanted to sit down and go over with you and your grandparents what to expect."

"Do you think he'll get it?"

"Not a lot of people get it on their first try, but your dad has done everything right that he can. He's been a model prisoner, and I know that it has a lot to do with the fact that you've never missed a visit."

"Well, every visit but one," Cass said, then took a sip of her iced tea.

The same week her mother died, she'd missed visitation, but that had been the only time. No matter how hard it was to see him like that, she never wanted to let him down, especially when Norm said regular visitations always helped prisoners keep their focus.

Prisoners who had no family or whose families ignored or abandoned them in prison often lost themselves on the inside. Norm told her the more families did to remind a loved one that the misery was only temporary, the more likely they were to serve a successful sentence and be considered rehabilitated.

"How soon could he be home?"

"Before Thanksgiving, if all goes well."

"Thank goodness. Maybe everyone will finally lose interest, and the reporters, like that one earlier, will go away for once and for all."

"What reporter?"

"Ty Thomas. He said he writes for the *Cumberland Press*, but I don't recall ever seeing his name in the paper. As soon as he figured out who I was, he wanted me to let him interview Nana and Pop Pop."

"That's perfect. That's just the kind of thing we could use to drum up positive press."

"I don't want anyone bothering my grandparents and dredging all this back up. They've been through enough."

"You need to think about this from the opposite side, Cassidy. If this reporter wants to do a story, especially one about how much your family has suffered, then it's bound to make people realize that your father has paid his debt and it's time to help your family do some healing by granting his parole and letting you all get on with your lives."

"Well, I already told him no, so that's that."

"I'd advise you to give it some additional thought. At least, let me talk to your grandparents, then, if they won't do it, we'll let it go."

Cass' stomach lurched, but not from hunger. She'd been short, if not out-and-out rude to Thomas. He probably didn't even *want* to do the story now.

Selby returned.

"What'll it be, folks?"

Norm nodded for Cass to go ahead.

"I'm really not very hungry."

"How 'bout a cup of soup?" Selby suggested. "I put on a pot of ham and bean this morning."

"Sure, that'd be fine."

"Oh, come on. You can do better than that," Norm said.

Cass shrugged at him. "I'll see if there's any room left after my soup."

"No wonder you're so little," Norm said, then looked to Selby. "Give me a cheeseburger and make it a double."

"You got it," Selby said and headed for the kitchen.

They spent the rest of the meal strategizing. Cass needed to get the family pastor to visit her dad and recruit him to write a recommendation to the parole board. The mayor and her father had gone to high school together, so he might help too.

Cass could barely finish her soup. So much work to do. It sounded just like farming, you planted seed after seed, poured in all your blood, sweat, and tears, then all you could do was hope and pray something would grow out of it.

She called Beth on the way home.

"You are not going to believe who has a hot date for Saturday night," her friend blurted into the phone without a word of greeting.

"With the reporter?"

"You know it."

"Are you sure you want to do that?"

"Why wouldn't I? You saw how gorgeous he is. Those eyes alone could melt butter at fifty paces."

Cass chose not to say anymore. As Pop Pop would say, the man had the aura of a snake oil salesman, and she cringed at what she was about to do.

"I'm sure you'll give me all the details. So did Casanova give you his phone number? You know, to follow up with him or to make date arrangements?"

"He sure did."

"Good. Will you text it to me? I actually have to call him and apologize."

"For what?"

"For reacting the way that I did when he asked about my dad."

"Seriously?"

"Not one of my prouder moments. I'm going to fix it, though, so just text me the number, okay?"

"Sure."

"Thanks. For now, I have to get home and get my knife and fork. I'm about to eat some humble pie."

Chapter Six

Cass walked up to the small desk where a short, round, brunette woman manned a constantly ringing telephone.

She handed a clipboard marked "Visitors' Log" for Cass to supply her name, Ty Thomas' name, the date, and the time.

The woman took back the clipboard, glanced at Cass' information, then turned to her computer and fired off what looked like an Instant Message, all while explaining to the caller that the local events section had to cover all local events fairly and was not just limited to the social events of First Baptist Church.

No sooner did she finish that call when another came in, and she immersed herself in explaining that just because the first score reported on the sports page was Central High not Cumberland Springs High did not mean the paper supported Central more.

"Cassidy French. I never would have imagined I'd see you again so soon."

Cass turned at the sound of Ty's voice and flashed him a smile that she really hoped came across as one part humble and another part sincere.

"Hi, Ty. I'm just as surprised as you are."

He reached out for her hand, and she shook his. His skin was warm, and his grip was firm but not forceful.

"I don't really have an office," he confessed, flashing her a smile brimming with charm. "How about we step into a conference room?"

"That'd be great."

She followed him down the hall and into a small room on the right. An oval table housed six chairs on rollers, and Ty waved toward the table.

"Take your pick."

She took the one closest to the door, while Ty took the one at the head of the table.

"I have to admit I was quite surprised by your call. I hope you know I didn't mean to cause any upset. It's just the newshound in me. The first thing that usually pops into my head is how I can turn something into a story, and I admit, that probably seemed insensitive to your family's plight."

He talked so fast, it made her dizzy.

"Well, I probably overreacted a little too. Reporters and busybodies absolutely hammered us when it first happened, then again a year later when the trial was going on. I guess I had a bit of a knee-jerk reaction as soon as you showed interest."

"How about we wipe the slate clean on both sides and call it even, then?"

Cass nodded. "I can handle that."

Ty pointed at the empty space in front of her. "Can I get you a drink or something? Cup of coffee?"

Cass shook her head. "Actually, I came here to ask you just what kind of interview you had in mind."

He made a good-natured shrug. "I haven't really done my homework. I'd have to see what's been written before, if anything.

"I just know that it would probably make an excellent human interest story. I mean, a tragedy like that, how does a family cope with it? How do they move on, or do they remain stuck in that moment for the rest of their lives?"

Cass cringed on the inside. Good luck getting Pop Pop to answer questions like that. His idea of a deep conversation was whether cornbread or buttermilk biscuits went better with Nana's pork chops.

Ty studied her in silence.

"If you're still worried about whether or not I'll be careful around your grandparents, I will be."

"It's not that—" She stopped herself. That was *exactly* what it was. "Well, just a little."

"Tell you what, I have to get over to the county line for another story I'm looking into. Why don't I pick you up for dinner, and we can talk about it, then? Say, seven o'clock?"

She blanched. That sounded a whole lot more like a date than an interview strategy session. First of all, she wasn't about to go out with another guy when she hadn't even figured out what was or wasn't going on with Mitch.

Second of all, Beth would have a hissy fit and a half if word got back to her that the date she had hoped to have with Mr. Dreamy had gone to Cass instead. Those gorgeous blue eyes had her locked in their sights like she was the first deer of open season, and she got a little nagging feeling that if Beth saw that look, she'd never hear the end of it.

"I usually eat a little earlier than that. If we're going to do this, why don't you come out to the house for dinner?"

His expression didn't change, but he looked up, apparently mulling it over. "I'll need a day or two to make some notes. How about if I call you?"

She gave him her cell number instead of the number at the farm. She needed to brace her grandparents for this development. Once they heard Norm's explanation, they'd be much more open to the idea, but until she or Norm got to talk to them, she didn't want them unintentionally fielding a phone call that got the same reaction out of them as it had her, initially.

"I'll walk you out to your truck, then. Just let me get my things."

She waited in the hallway. Along both walls hung several black and white photos from throughout the county. She recognized some of the faces. There was a picture of the new courthouse being built. There was a picture of the collapsed covered bridge on County Line Road. Another picture showed a farmer making rolls of hay, and still another picture showed three little boys dressed like rodeo clowns riding a bale of hay like it was a horse. One of the little boys even had his hand tucked under the binding and waved a cowboy hat in the air.

Ty rejoined her in the hall, this time with a black messenger's satchel slung over one shoulder. They smiled at one another, and she turned and walked toward the parking lot. He followed closely.

"Have you ever lived anywhere else but Cumberland Springs?" he asked as they headed toward her truck.

"Just school. I went to MTSU for a year and a half before Mamma got sick, and I had to come home."

"Are you going to go back?"

"Probably not. I figure I know enough to get by, for now anyways. Time will tell, though."

She climbed into the truck, and he closed the door behind her.

Her window was still down, and she leaned her arm against it.

"Is that your answer to everything? Time will tell?"

She thought about it. "It hasn't failed me yet."

He looked out over the other cars parked throughout the lot then fixed his gaze on her again. "You sure you wouldn't rather meet for dinner and talk about the interview first?"

"I'll think about it. How's that?"

"Better than your first answer."

With a wink, he stepped back from the truck, and she started the engine.

All the way home, her mind bounced from topic to topic. So many things fought for attention. If she approached this interview the right way, her father might be home for the holidays. If she approached Mitch the right way, she might have a boyfriend by then too.

Funny how life never let you cruise along at the same steady pace. No, life liked to play feast or famine with you. It either threatened to drown you in too many things to deal with at once, or it made you worry that you were going to starve to death, sometimes literally and sometimes only emotionally.

When she pulled up the driveway, she recognized Norm's shiny, navy-blue Buick. She climbed down from the truck and shoved her keys into her pocket. Her fingers brushed the folded check from Marie. Darn. She'd have to go back into town again to deposit it. Later, though.

For now, she headed into the kitchen. Time to tackle this interview thing head-on.

Chapter Seven

"Sounds to me like you don't like this Ty Thomas fella very much," Nana said the next evening as they prepared a big dinner for themselves and Ty.

Apparently his research hadn't taken as long as he'd thought it would, and he was ready to talk to them after only a day.

Cass picked up green beans out of one colander, snapped them, then dropped them into a separate colander while Nana peeled potatoes.

"Oh, he's very likable. He'll charm the pants off you, if you let him. If anything, he's *too* charming."

Their hands moved in synchronicity, creating a steady rhythm of snapping and scraping sounds.

"You know," Nana said without looking up from her

potato peeling, "we should have Mitchell over for Sunday supper. He doesn't work Sundays, does he?"

"I'm not sure," Cass replied, looking harder than she really had to at her pile of green beans. Juggling Ty and Mitch in the same conversation would probably make her head explode.

"Well, you should ask him."

"I'll think about it, Nana."

Pop Pop clip-clopped down the wooden stairs in his Sunday suit and dress shoes. He had parted his hair on the left side and slicked it into place, and he looked as nervous as a first-time preacher about to step into the pulpit.

Cass whistled at him, and Nana looked up and smiled. "Well, if you aren't just the handsomest thing."

He managed a tight-lipped smile, and Cass had to look harder into her bowl of beans to keep from laughing. The man could solve just about any problem in the field, could hold his own in a debate or argument with any livestock judge in the state, but bring up something even remotely emotional, and he lost the power of speech.

Cass finished snapping the beans and wiped her hands on the towel in her lap.

"You want me to go ahead and put these on the stove, Nana?"

"Let them soak until the potatoes are done."

Cass stacked the full colander inside the empty one,

and carried everything into the kitchen. She dumped the green beans into a pan, added water, and left them to soak on an unlit stove eye.

Pop Pop followed her and poured a glass of water. He drank until he'd emptied it.

Cass walked over behind him and wrapped her arms around his shoulders. She touched her forehead to his right shoulder blade.

"This is going to help Daddy."

He didn't say anything, but he reached up and patted along her forearm. They stood that way until Nana brought the potatoes in.

"I'll change, and then I'll help you finish," Cass said.

"Take your time, dear. I'll put this good-looking man to work setting the table."

Cass prepped as fast as she could. She unbraided her hair, shook it, and combed through it loosely with her fingers. The thick brown waves hung down past her shoulders. She pulled the sides up and used a small black squeeze clip to secure them in the back. She changed into chocolate-brown slacks and a green blouse and slipped into some brown leather ballet-style flats, the most comfortable shoes ever.

She applied a small amount of base to even out her skin tone, but she didn't add any other makeup. She wanted to look presentable but didn't want to fuel romantic notions of any sort.

She added her mother's gold stud earrings, then checked herself in the mirror. *Ready or not, here we go*, she thought and made her way back toward the kitchen.

As she crossed the drive, a pair of headlights zeroed in on Cass like a spotlight. She stood and waited. The vehicle that pulled up was a large, dark-colored Ford truck, just like the one Mitch drove.

His unmistakable silhouette got out of the truck and came toward her.

"Aren't you a sight for sore eyes. You look gorgeous," he said as he closed the distance between them.

"Hey, stranger," she said, feeling the smile spread across her face. Had she really been *worried* about asking him out?

The floodlights came on, smothering them in light so bright, they each put a hand up to shield their eyes.

"What brings you out this way?" she asked.

Once her eyes adjusted, she gave him a good looking-over. He had on dark blue jeans and a burgundy button-down shirt, with the top button unbuttoned. She'd gotten so used to seeing him in uniform, she had forgotten what he looked like without it.

The nerves and hesitation over Ty's impending visit fell away, and a wave of excitement replaced them, especially when she caught a whiff of Stetson on the breeze.

"I thought you might like to go for a ride. Thought we could pick up some ice cream from Turner's and drive around town."

Inside, she swooned, and she hated what she had to say next.

"Aw, Mitch, I'd love to, but we're havin' company tonight."

Another pair of headlights came up the drive, and Cass clenched her jaw. Bad enough that she had to miss such a delightful-sounding outing with Mitch, but Ty couldn't have picked a worse time to arrive.

The headlights belonged to a Jeep that chugged to a stop beside Cass' silver truck.

"Okay. I have to say this really fast before he gets out of the car."

"He? He who?"

"Shush, and I'll tell you. This guy's Ty Thomas, a reporter for the *Cumberland Press*. He's doing a story on what happened to Daddy."

"What? There's no story there anymore. That's old news."

"He wants to do some kind of behind-the-scenes thing to talk about what this did to the family, what's happened to us as a result, how we coped, that sort of thing."

"Your grandparents would never go for that. That's crazy."

Ty got out of the Jeep and walked around to the passenger side.

Cass whispered, "Norm Greer thinks it's a good idea. Daddy's up for parole soon, and an article like that might raise public interest in helping him come home, so Norm talked Pop Pop into doing it."

Ty approached them. His satchel hung from his right shoulder, and in his left hand he held a large bouquet full of daisies and chrysanthemums.

"Hi there," he said then flashed that smile of pure charm.

Cass returned a milder version of it then gestured between the two men.

"Ty Thomas, this is Mitch Riley."

"Here, hold these," Ty said, handing the flowers to Cass.

Ty and Mitch shook hands. At first glance, it appeared perfectly normal, but they didn't let go right away. Were they . . . having a stare-down? She had no idea what was going on between those two grips.

She looked at the large bunch of flowers in front of her and did her best not to look impressed. She'd never been given flowers before.

Ty must've noticed something in her expression. He looked at her funny then added, "They're for your grandmother. I know this isn't exactly a social visit, but I thought they might smooth the waters a little."

"I'll take them right to her," Cass said and did her best not to sound too relieved. The last thing she wanted was for Mitch to see some stranger giving her flowers and to get the wrong idea.

The screen door creaked open, and all three of them turned toward the sound. Cass' grandparents came down the porch steps.

Before they'd even reached the last stair, Cass could see exactly what would happen. Nana would see Mitch and invite him to stay for dinner. For the entire meal, Mitch and Ty would keep up their little competition. There would be no interview, and she and her grandparents would have to go through this all over again in a day or two.

"Can I talk to you a sec?" Cass asked Mitch, hooking her arm through his and pulling him to the back of the truck.

Ty could handle himself with her grandparents for a minute. If nothing else, that boy knew how to talk.

"I don't like him," Mitch said, none too quietly, his eyes practically burning a hole through the back of Ty's head.

"Gee, I hadn't noticed," Cass said then smirked.

"Look, I need this chance to help my father. Ever since that night, I've had to stand by and watch helplessly while all these terrible things happened to my family, while other people made decisions that changed my life forever, and I had *no* say at all."

Mitch finally turned his attention to her, and the hardness in his face disappeared.

"Tonight, Nana, Pop Pop, and I get a chance to do something to help. You know Nana's gonna take one look at you and ask you to stay. But don't. Please."

They stood there, eyes locked on one another.

Cass blinked first. "Nana wanted me to invite you to supper, Sunday, after church. How about if you give me a raincheck for ice cream and a long drive after that?"

He looked down at her with such a disapproving look, she was afraid he wasn't going to go for it.

"Please?" she added.

He took one more look toward Ty and her grandparents. His lips compressed until there was only a thin line where his mouth was.

She glanced at Ty and her grandparents. She tried to see what Mitch must see, a handsome stranger all smooth-talking and moving in on territory that, by all rights and respects, should be Mitch's.

He was probably thinking about how he didn't know the man, didn't know what he was capable of. One thing all good lawmen needed to be able to do was assess the level of threat. They didn't like unknowns.

Ty Thomas was definitely an unknown.

She gave Mitch her most pleading look. "You want to know the truth?"

His eyes met hers, and his resolve wavered for the briefest moment.

"You're a distraction to me, a delicious, wonderful, welcome distraction, but a distraction just the same."

A crease appeared in the center of his forehead. Maybe she hadn't said that right.

"All I mean is that I have to have my mind sharp. I'm not going to lie to him, but my answers have to be the best they can be."

"Maybe I can help," he offered, then smiled weakly. They both knew better than that.

"Come to supper Sunday, and I will clear my calendar just for you."

"And I better get the entire square."

He had a set to his jaw that meant business.

"Cross my heart," she said, and moved her index finger in the criss-cross motion over the left side of her chest.

Nana called to them, "So, Cassidy, are you going to invite these fine young men in to dinner or not?"

Cass flashed one last pleading look at Mitch then turned around. "Mitch just needed to tell me something. He's on his way back out."

"She's right, Mrs. French, I need to get going. I'm sure you made a fine dinner, though, and I'm sorry to miss it. Maybe another time."

Cass turned around and stood on her tip-toes to reach Mitch's ear.

"Thanks," she whispered, then gave him a quick peck on the cheek.

Nana always knew how to set a perfect table, and tonight was no exception. The family china and silverware shimmered and sparkled like a setting from an elegant living magazine. The smell of pork tenderloin that had simmered all afternoon filled the air, and Cass licked her lips.

She helped carry over the gravy for the mashed potatoes and the serving bowl of steamed carrots. Both Ty and Pop Pop stood respectfully beside their chairs.

Only after Cass and her grandmother had taken their seats did the men slide into their own chairs. White linen napkins disappeared into laps, and everyone started loading plates and passing dishes.

"I only get to eat like this during the holidays," Ty said,

"You're not married?" Nana asked.

"I'm afraid not. I dated a few different girls in college, but once I started working . . ." he said, taking a couple of dinner rolls from the bread basket then passing it to Pop Pop. "Well, reporting isn't like a lot of jobs. The hours aren't regular. The pay is usually pretty lousy. It's kind of hard to get a relationship going."

"Well, that's too bad for such a nice boy like you," Nana said.

"Eh, it comes when it's supposed to," Pop Pop chimed in.

Cass glanced across the table and caught Ty staring at her. Pop Pop passed the rolls to her, and she welcomed the opportunity to turn her attention away from Ty.

She'd already apologized for her reaction and

agreed to get him his interview. Why would he still pour on the Casanova eyes?

They danced around a variety of polite topics throughout the meal, but when the last dinner roll was gone, Pop Pop dropped his napkin onto his plate and pushed his chair back. He looked at Ty.

"I hear you got some questions about my boys. You wanna know what that accident's done to my family. Not much to say about that. It's done what you'd think it'd do, tore it up one side and down the other. I put one boy in the ground, and I watched another go off to jail.

"I'm gonna tell you somethin'. A man does what's asked of him. I served in Vietnam, and it didn't take some draft to get me there, neither. I did my time, and I came home, and lotsa folks around here didn't. And don't you think for one minute that that thought doesn't cross my mind every day.

"My boys made a mistake that night. Both of 'em did. But Hank Jr. owed up to what happened, and he's doin' his time. And when he comes home, we'll deal with what we gotta deal with. And that's all I've gotta say."

He stood up, and Ty fixed a respect-filled gaze on him. "Thank you, Mr. French. I appreciate your taking the time to talk to me."

Then Pop Pop did the last thing Cass ever expected him to. He reached out and shook Ty's hand, then he went out the back door.

Over a freshly baked cherry pie, Nana and Cass offered considerable more detailed answers than what Pop Pop had given. They talked about all the missed holidays and milestones. Each of them choked up when they described the difficulty of trying to cope with their own grief yet still comfort a man who missed the last two years of his wife's life.

Two more hours passed surprisingly quickly, but Cass felt drained and exhausted as she walked Ty to his Jeep.

"I can't get over how strong and close your family is, Cass," he said, loading his bag back into the passenger seat.

"We're just us," she said with a shrug.

"Well, I had a really nice evening with you and your family tonight. I know you were worried about how this would go, and I promised I would be as sensitive as possible. I hope I didn't disappoint you."

She had to admit he had lived up to his promise. He hadn't pushed her grandfather once he'd said all he was going to say.

"I can easily say it was the most pleasant one of these interviews so far."

"It's the only one of these interviews you've done, isn't it?"

"Well, yeah." Cass looked away with a guilty grin.

"Cass, look at me," he said in a soft voice.

She did as he asked and noticed that he had stepped even closer to her.

"If it's not too much to ask, I'd really like to see you again."

She gulped.

"Let me guess . . . the deputy guy? Is he really your boyfriend?"

Cass bit her lip. How was she supposed to explain her and Mitch to some stranger? "No, he's not my boyfriend, but it's complicated."

Ty's gaze held a potent mix of intensity and reassurance. She couldn't help but stare.

"Maybe the time is right for something simpler in your life?"

He leaned forward and tilted his head, and panic flurried through her body.

She turned her head to the side, and his lips met her cheek instead of their intended target.

"I'm sorry," she whispered. "I don't mean to be rude. I just . . . things are just—"

"Complicated?"

She turned her head back, so she could face him, and nodded.

He hadn't stepped back, and their noses were only a fraction of an inch apart. The nearness filled her with one part exhilaration and one part apprehension.

"I'm actually looking forward to reading your article," she said in a thinly veiled subject change. "I can't wait to tell my dad how we're trying to help when I see him Friday."

"This Friday? As in, day after tomorrow?" Ty

asked with that same perkiness in his voice that had started all this mess in the first place.

Cass nodded.

"You still visit him?"

"Every first Friday of the month. I've only ever missed it once."

"That's great. Would you let me come with you?"

The bottom dropped out of Cass' stomach.

"I don't know," she said, looking off in the distance to avoid those eager eyes. "Visitation days are hard."

"I think this would really add even more depth to the story, especially if I can get some pictures."

"I'll think about it," Cass said slowly.

"Great. I'll call you tomorrow."

He bounded around the Jeep to the driver's side, and Cass turned and walked back to the kitchen. Nana needed help with the dishes, and she needed advice. Lots of it.

Chapter Eight

The next morning, Cass was on her way to the barn from the hog pens when her cell phone rang. The number was Beth's, and her friend didn't even give her a greeting before jumping into the real purpose of the call.

"So how did the interview go?"

"I finally figured out who Ty reminds me of."

"Oh I can't wait to hear this."

"Rhett Butler."

Beth cackled into the phone.

"Hear me out. He just oozes all this charm and appeal, but when he zeroes in on something, you might as well give up. He's going to get what he wants, and whether he has to charm you to death, or engage you in some sort of debate, he's got this endless amount of energy and determination to go after it, either way."

"Sheesh. I thought you were making a joke, but that's pretty dead-on."

Cass tried to figure out how to break the near-kiss to her friend.

Cass took a deep breath and kept going. "The questions part was all right. Pop Pop gave him one statement, then declared he was done. And Ty was actually nice enough about it to let him go."

"He's such a sweetie."

"You might not think so when I tell you about the walk to the car."

"Uh oh."

Cass bit the bullet. "He asked to see me again. Just me. Like a date. And then he tried to kiss me."

Beth didn't say a word.

The silence was so heavy, Cass cringed for fear of what must be going through her best bud's mind.

"I didn't encourage it. I turned my head."

"Isn't it enough you've got the Mitch stuff going on? It's not like there's an unlimited supply of bachelors in this town."

Cass cleared her throat. "I told you I didn't encourage it. He just did it, Beth. I'm sorry. I really am. I know you had hopes and all."

Beth sighed. "Well, crap. Now I'm back to hoping that we get cute interns next summer."

Cass tried to think up some quick damage control. "You could be his rebound girl, you know. After I shot him down and all."

Ever the optimist, Beth latched onto that idea. "Oooh, I like the sound of that."

"So, what are the odds you could get tomorrow off of work?"

"Tomorrow? I'll have to check my calendar for tours or VIPs. Why?"

"He wants to go with me to visitation day."

"What? Why?"

"He thinks it'll make a better story. He's going to try to take pictures, although good luck getting that past security with no advance notice."

"So why don't you call them and give them advance notice?"

"Hey, I'm not the reporter here. He should do his homework."

"What'll they do to him?"

"Lock him up," Cass said with a grin.

Beth gasped.

"Not really. Probably just make him wait out in the truck. Serves him right for barging into our lives like that. Besides, with such short notice, I won't get a chance to warn my dad, and he'll flip his lid if I show up to visitation with cameras and a reporter."

"You're so mean." Beth clucked her tongue. "Yup, sounds like that boy is going to need some of my special healing, all right."

"Go for it," Cass said, making her way past the barn and toward her little above–garage apartment. "All right, I've got coding to do. Call me back when you find out whether you can get tomorrow off or not."

"Will do."

They hung up at the same time. Cass pulled off her boots and left them on the mat beside the door to her apartment. She grabbed a can of Mountain Dew from the extra fridge and walked up the stairs to her computer and some distraction from this drama.

She slipped out of her jeans and pulled on some sweats. She paused for a moment then walked over to the armoire. She reached inside and pulled Mitch's sweatshirt from the bottom of it.

She had just changed shirts and rolled up the sleeves when her cell phone rang again. She didn't recognize the number on the display.

"This is Cassidy French."

"Hey, Cass, it's Ty."

Ugh. Not the voice she wanted to hear right now.

"Hello, Ty. What's new?"

"I'm driving out to County Line Road to finish up an assignment, and I thought I'd call and check in with you while I was on my way. What're your thoughts about tomorrow?"

Cass popped the top on the soda can and took a long drink. Tell him no, and she wouldn't have to worry about anything else. Tell him yes, and she'd have the satisfaction of seeing him sent back to the parking lot to wait while she got to visit with her dad.

"I suppose you could come along. I leave early, though. You'd need to be here by seven, at the latest."

"Not a problem."

"See you then."

She ended the call and crossed her fingers that Beth would come through, and she wouldn't have to face him alone.

Chapter Nine

Cassidy French had just opened her eyes when she realized what day this was. She quickly closed them again and rolled over. Cecil mewed in protest at the interruption, clamped onto her foot, and rabbit-kicked her.

"Sorry," she said and rolled the other way.

She bowed her head and pulled the neck of the sweatshirt back enough to dip her nose inside it. She had to take a really deep breath to pick up any trace of Mitch's Stetson. Another day or two, and she wouldn't be able to tell it had been there at all.

Two days from now, they'd have their first date in years. Had he thought about that when he first woke up this morning too?

Although . . . what if all his kindness was just his

way of taking pity on her? How could a man who loved the law and organization and all the things that went with them find her and her messed up family even remotely attractive?

Sure, they'd been infatuated with one another when they were teenagers, but now . . . now, she was just another good deed waiting to be worked. Surely, he viewed her as just some fixer-upper opportunity.

Her days were filled with chores and livestock and just enough coding to eke out a meager existence. His days were filled with saving lives and making the world a safer place.

She hid from the world, while he patrolled it.

Totally wrong for one another.

She groaned, threw the covers back, and rolled out of bed. The whole point of snuggling back under the blanket had been to build up her energy reserves to face this day, especially since Beth hadn't been able to get the day off. Instead of feeling better, all she had managed to do was brew up a bunch of over-analyzing that actually made her feel worse.

Cass hit the shower and went through her routine for visitation day. As always, the simpler, the better. She did a quick French braid, wore light makeup, and went without any jewelry. She chose a thin pink turtleneck sweater and pocketless black slacks with it. She hated dressing like a frumpy old maid, but she learned her lesson on her first visit. If she gave the guards as few things to check for as possible, she could get through the security checkpoints that much faster and get to the most important part, seeing her father.

She slipped on simple black ballet-style flats, then checked herself in the mirror hanging on the back of her bedroom door. She frowned. She fidgeted with the sweater. She unbraided and re-braided her hair, even though it came out the exact same way. Despite having done this dozens and dozens of times, and even though she knew Ty most likely wouldn't be intruding on her visit, nerves plagued her more than usual.

Her father was a lot more like Pop Pop than he ever cared to admit. He wouldn't want to talk about his time in prison or the night of the accident. He had never offered an explanation for why he and Uncle Richie had been racing one another, so he certainly wouldn't open up to some stranger now.

He wouldn't be very happy that she and Nana had actually given interviews, either. Although, if he got paroled and came home early, she suspected that might change his tune.

After gathering the eggs, she headed toward the house. Nana had breakfast going in the kitchen. The smell of bacon and freshly baked biscuits greeted her as she wiped her feet on the mat at the back door.

"Mornin', Nana," Cass called from the entryway.

"There she is. I told you she'd be along shortly."

Cass poked her head around the wall and into the kitchen. There, at the dining table, sat Ty.

"Good morning, Miss French," Ty said.

"Hello, Mr. Thomas."

What is he doing here so early?

She ducked back behind the wall to buy some time for herself by adjusting the eggs in the basket.

After a moment she brought the eggs into the kitchen and set the basket down on the end of the counter. When she turned around, Ty was watching her.

"I couldn't get a photographer for a trip like this on such short notice, so it's just me today. I wanted to make sure I didn't hold you up, so I came over early. Your grandmother was kind enough to invite me in for breakfast."

Nana tsked as she pulled out a tray of biscuits from inside the stove. "He called that thing his breakfast."

She pointed at a wrapped fruit bar near the coffeepot.

Cass made an exaggerated wince at Ty. "Bad move. As far as Nana's concerned, you don't cut corners at mealtime. You always eat three a day, and they're always hot."

Nana began muttering about make-it-in-a-minute meals and drink mixes that were supposed to take the place of food. She brought the bread basket over to the table.

"I remember when they introduced that orange

drink mix that was supposed to take the place of juice, oh, and that astronaut ice cream. Sugar-coated cardboard, that's all it was. And of course, your dad and Richie were just crazy about it. Every trip into town, they'd beg for it."

Cass silently walked over and grabbed three juice glasses. Nana always brought up Daddy and Uncle Richie stories on visitation day. Cass set the glasses at each of their places at the table. She got the pitcher of apple juice from the refrigerator and carried it over to the table, then she took her place across from Ty.

"Where's your husband?" Ty asked.

"He's not going to eat right now. He'll eat with the boys a little later," Nana said.

Wordlessly, Nana and Cass added food to their plates.

Cass could feel Ty's stare, but she didn't look up at him. She added just a little sliver of butter to her biscuit then put it aside to melt. She sprinkled pepper over the small mound of scrambled eggs.

She studied the black and silver specks that dotted the fluffy yellow and white landscape. She didn't know how long she stared at them like that, but it must have been a couple of minutes because Nana interrupted her thinking.

"Best eat before it gets cold, dear."

Cass looked over at her just as Nana reached for her hand. Nana's soft, warm fingers curled over the tops of her own, and Cass felt a lump in her throat. She bent down and kissed the back of Nana's hand.

Tears glistened in Nana's eyes. She stood up and stepped closer to Cass.

"You eat up, now. I feel a touch of a headache comin' on, so I'm going to lie down for a minute. Leave your dishes, and I'll get them when your grandpa and the boys come in."

Nana kissed Cass on the head then walked out of the dining room.

"Did I say something wrong?" Ty asked.

Cass swallowed hard, willing the lump in her throat to go back down. She stood and carried her plate to the counter. She got the roll of aluminum foil out of a drawer by the sink. She snapped a strip of bacon into thirds, then she took her fork and scooped some of the scrambled egg into the biscuit, added the bacon, building her own little version of a breakfast sandwich. She wrapped it in some aluminum foil.

"Bring me your plate, and I'll wrap up your breakfast," she said.

Ty did as she asked, and she did the same with his food.

"Did I say something wrong?" he repeated.

"No. It's just today. Pop Pop doesn't eat breakfast with me because I always ask him to go, but he never does. And the one time Nana went, she fainted at the security checkpoint. It's just too much for them. I gotta get Daddy home. I just gotta get Daddy home."

Ty put a hand on her shoulder and turned her toward him.

She looked into his eyes, and he looked directly into hers, only this time, with more determination than desire.

"I promise to do whatever I can to help make that happen."

"Thanks."

Her lips twitched into something she hoped resembled a smile.

Ty reached around her, and she tensed.

He took a step back, and when he brought his hands back around, he had the two bundles of aluminum foil.

"Ready?"

"Sure," she said with a certainty she didn't feel in the least.

It took her another deep breath before she could relax her shoulders. The good thing about taking breakfast with them was that, if she ate slowly enough, she could avoid conversation for almost half the trip.

One thought always struck Cass as she moved through the prison's concrete and tile hallways on her way from the security checkpoint into Riverbend's main visitation gallery. The hallways of a prison and the hallways of a hospital were a lot alike. Desperation and hopelessness tainted the air so thickly, you could feel it clinging to you, almost like you were walking through a mist.

Just as she had hoped, Ty had not been allowed through security. She'd been able to walk on through, leaving him behind as he tried to charm the corrections officers into letting him speak directly with the warden. She didn't care who they let him talk to so long as she did not have to endure the added burden of making this walk and feeling this pain with someone there trying to document it all.

Two sets of prisoners and visitors occupied the far corners of the primary visitation room, so Cass took a table near the center. She folded her hands in her lap and made a conscious effort to take deep, slow breaths. Calm and composed would be the best way to break this many items of news to her father.

The door creaked open, and Cass looked up, pushing her lips into a big smile so she could greet her father warmly. A guard held the door open, but, instead of her father, Ty walked in. Cass began to grind her teeth.

He made a beeline for her. "Did I miss it? Have you seen him yet?"

"They haven't brought him in yet."

She stood up.

"How did you get in here?"

"My quick wit and charm?"

She smirked.

"I have press credentials that they could verify, and they make exceptions for visitors who travel great distances or have extenuating circumstances, even if they aren't on the individual prisoner's visitation list."

Cass clenched her jaw tighter. Ty was supposed to be back in the truck by now. She was supposed to have a free and easy visit with her dad.

"Can't you wait outside until I get a chance to talk to him?"

"And miss the reunion shot? No way. That will make a great picture."

Cass sighed and looked toward the door. Daddy would be upset enough that she had press here, but he'd totally flip out if he were bushwhacked during a tender moment.

"What if I get him to agree to a farewell hug in front of the camera?"

"I don't want something that looks too staged."

She grabbed his hand and squeezed it. "Please. Please understand. He doesn't know you're coming. Visitation days are bittersweet, at best. If he feels ambushed or tricked, he's going to be mad at you, me, the whole place. Give me a few minutes to get him used to the idea, then I'll get you a farewell shot."

Ty looked like he wanted to continue to argue.

Cass didn't give him the chance. "If he gets mad over this, it might mess up future visitation, maybe even his parole. And the only thing you're going to be reporting is more tragedy."

"All right, all right."

Ty backed up and moved out the door.

When he was out of sight, Cass dropped down into a seat and put her head in her hands. That had been close.

Her breathing had just calmed down, when the door creaked again. Cass looked up to see her father walk into the room. His hair had grayed even more and seemed thinner than she remembered. He looked paler than she had ever seen him, and he moved forward with noticeable effort.

So broken, she thought and doubled her resolve to give him all the positive energy she could. That wouldn't be as hard this visit as it had been for others. She actually had some good news this time, but the probable negative reaction to Ty's presence made his overall reaction hard to guess.

"Hi, Daddy," she said, sliding onto her feet and taking a step toward him. She wrapped her arms around his waist and hugged him.

He made a gruff-sounding snort, but his arms went around her, anyway. While she didn't have an exact measurement, she felt pretty sure his hug was tighter.

"I thought I told you to stop wasting your time here," he said sourly.

"I'm glad to see you, too," Cass said much more sweetly than she felt.

She stepped back, and they studied one another.

"Look at my pretty little girl."

Touches weren't allowed to go on very long, so they sat down, opposite from one another at the table.

"How're you feeling, Daddy? How are you doing?"

He shrugged. "Been better. Been worse."

He always said that. Just like all the times before, it never really told her much of anything.

"So why do you keep coming back here? Why can't you just leave me here to rot like everyone else has?"

"No one's left you here to rot, Dad. We're just anxious for you to be home again."

He frowned.

"It's true. I actually need to talk to you about that. Has Norm been to see you, or has he called you about your parole hearing?"

"He might've mentioned it," he said with a shrug and looked at the other groups of visitors.

"Well, there are a lot of things we can do to help make your case as strong as possible for the parole board. I'm working on a few things now."

"Cassidy, I don't want you doing anything about this stuff. You just leave it to me and Norm."

"The same duo who shot up an outhouse they thought was a bear on their first hunting trip?"

Her father laughed so suddenly and so loudly, she jumped. After several moments, he started coughing and wheezing.

Eventually, her father regained his composure, and sat back down at the table. Cass went to the guard working the door.

"Could I buy some water for him?"

He nodded, and she gave him the money. He returned in a minute with the bottle. She took it back to the table and handed her father the bottle of water.

"Here, Daddy."

The guard returned to the door, and Cass took a seat across from her dad.

"Don't start," he said as he uncapped the water bottle.

"Don't they have doctors in here? How long has this been going on?"

He didn't answer the question but took a long drink of water, instead.

She tried to remember her last visit and how he had seemed then. She didn't recall him having any coughing fits, but they hadn't shared any real laughter during her last visit, either. Like most visits, the majority of the conversation had been her giving him the gossip from home and him refusing to share with her any details about life inside.

She decided to shelve any more discussion of his health and filed away the topic for her next call or lunch with Norm.

"Seriously, Dad, I need to talk to you about a project I'm working on to help with your parole hearing."

"Yeah? What's that?"

"I did an interview with a reporter."

"You did what?"

"Well it was all of us, really. Nana, Pop Pop, and I."

"My father gave a reporter an interview? Did hell freeze over while I was in here?"

Cass smiled. "No. We just all want you home, and we're willing to do whatever it takes to help, even if it means that Pop Pop has to give a statement to the press."

Her dad took another long and contemplative drink.

"Anyway, as part of the story, the reporter actually came here with me today to get a picture of us together."

"Forget that."

He got up from the table and looked around the room.

"Daddy, please. Sit back down."

He muttered some things she felt pretty thankful she couldn't hear, if his expression were any indication.

She stood up and gave him the biggest doe eyes she could manage. "Don't you understand how important this is? Even Pop Pop got in on it."

He put his left hand up to his forehead and rubbed at his temples with such energy, he looked like he was trying to dig the irritation out, rather than just alleviate some pressure.

"They don't let people like me out."

"Actually, you're the *exact* kind of person who

should be let out. No criminal record prior, full of remorse for what happened, no problems since then—"

"I don't deserve it," he said bitterly. "Just let whatever is meant to happen, happen."

"Don't you want to come home to us? Don't you want to get out of here?'

He looked at her with dull, empty eyes. He coughed twice, and his gaze seemed to dim even more.

"This was Norm's idea. He said it would help make a good impression on the community, maybe even the parole board."

"Anything else you want to talk about?"

A tightness crept across her chest. How could he *want* to stay in here? How could he *choose* this place over their family?

Pain and confusion twisted within her, adding to the tightness in her chest. She loved him so much, she came here month after month. She sat down with a reporter she didn't trust and opened up a part of herself, just to help him. She even twisted Pop Pop's arm into opening himself too. That's how much they *all* loved her father.

Didn't he love them back enough just to stand there for a picture, maybe even answer a couple of questions himself?

"Guess I'm done for this visit," Cass said and stood up.

"I'll see you next month, then," he replied, rising with her.

"I'll be at your parole hearing before then."

He shook his head. "I don't want you there. I mean it. You leave this to Norm. It's what he's here for."

"Daddy, I'm trying to help. Norm says all this is going to help."

"I don't need your help."

He stared at her with those empty eyes, and the heaviness in her chest sank into her stomach.

He added, "I don't *want* your help."

"You can't really mean that," she said hoarsely.

He stood up. "I mean it."

He leaned down and kissed the top of her head.

"Give Mamma my love," he said, then turned and walked toward the guard at the door.

Cassidy's lower lip twitched. Tears were imminent. She could feel them, a watery heaviness building in her eyes. She put her head against her forearm and let them fall.

Before long, she heard footsteps approach.

"Let me guess. He wasn't feeling particularly photogenic?" Ty asked from her left side.

She shook her head but didn't lift it. She felt the flat of what was probably Ty's hand on her back, between her shoulder blades. He patted her a few times.

"Let's go to the truck. We have to leave now that your dad is gone."

She straightened, but he didn't move his hand away. She wiped her eyes on the back of her hand before looking at Ty.

"Hey, you gonna be all right?"

She didn't answer his question. "I'm sorry you didn't get your picture."

He flashed her that thousand-watt smile. "Don't worry about it."

She walked to the door and went through checkout as fast as she could. She only answered questions by nodding or shaking her head and did everything she could to keep it together until she made it into the truck.

She leaned forward, resting her forehead against the rim of the steering wheel, and she finally let loose. She sobbed so hard, she could barely hear Ty open the passenger door, but she definitely felt the minor rocking of the truck when he climbed in.

She reached into the glove box and pulled out a couple of thin, papery, fast-food napkins. She wiped the tears away, blew her nose, then shoved the napkins under the seat.

"He doesn't want any help," she said when she could catch her breath at last. "He sounds like he doesn't even care if he gets parole or not. It's like he wants to stay in there and rot forever."

Ty didn't say anything. He simply reached over and rubbed her back again. After a few moments, he curled his fingers over the round of her left shoulder and pulled her into him. He put both arms around her and leaned his lips against the side of her head.

"I'm sorry he can't see the wonderful things you're doing to help him," he said into her hair.

She stopped thinking about her father for a moment and summed up what was going on between Ty and her. She would have given anything for this to be Mitch instead.

Today was only Friday, though, so she had two more days before church and their outing afterwards. At this rate, she'd be a sniffling lump in *no* shape for the dating do-over they'd finally been granted by the powers that be.

"Thanks, Ty. I'll be all right."

She pulled back, but he didn't let go right away. She pulled a little harder, and he released her.

"You sure don't want to let anyone in do you?" Ty asked.

"I just . . ."

She sighed. "Today is a bad day, and I'm sorry if I'm not myself. I appreciate your kindness, Ty."

She looked him square in the eyes. "I really do."

"What is it, exactly?" he asked, and she thought she could detect a wounded quality to his voice. "Do you not trust anyone, or is it just me?"

"I really don't wanna talk about this now," she said and started the truck. "Are you hungry?"

"Please, Cassidy. I'm not a bad guy."

"I didn't say you were," she replied, buckling her seat belt.

Through the windshield she could see acres and acres of shiny silver fencing, topped with dazzlingly brilliant coils of silver razor-wire. The sunlight gleamed and shimmered within the metal spirals, but the sight made her shiver.

Despite the oddly beautiful way they gleamed in the sunlight, they would tear someone to pieces.

"We keep our cows more humanely than this place keeps people," she said.

"What?"

Cassidy put the truck in gear. "Are you hungry? There's a nice little pizza place near here."

Ty let out a sigh that sounded full of frustration and shoved his camera into his bag then pushed it under the seat.

Cass pulled out of the parking space and started them on the long road home.

"I don't know a single person that moping has ever helped," Nana said from the doorway to Cass' room.

Cass raised her head off her pillow, looked over at her grandmother, then put her head back down.

Nana walked in and sat beside her on the bed.

"Bad visit with your father, dear?"

"He told me to send you his love."

"How'd he seem?"

"He had a pretty bad cough."

"Has he seen a doctor?"

"He didn't say. He kind of avoided the question."

"Your father always was good at wiggling out of a discussion. Your grandpa and I used to think he was going to be a lawyer just like Norm."

Cass sat up. *Norm.* That was a great idea. He would be the best chance at help for her father now that the newspaper article was down the drain since Ty had gotten no picture or interview with her father.

"I know what would make you feel better. How about I whip up some banana pudding for after dinner tonight?"

Nana's banana pudding could cure any number of ills. Heck, if they'd just send any of Nana's desserts over to the Middle East, they'd probably get an immediate ceasefire.

"I'm kind of working on plans for dinner, but some of your banana pudding sounds like heaven. I'll save plenty of room."

"So."

Cass didn't like the little lilt in Nana's voice as she prepared for a subject change.

"Would your dinner plans include a certain deputy we all know?"

"Not this time, Nana. I did remember to invite him to Sunday supper after church. He'll be there."

"He's such a nice boy."

Cass smiled. Mitch had stopped being a boy long ago, but the warmth and approval in Nana's voice was unmistakable.

"Well, you let me know about dinner, and I'll make sure your grandfather doesn't eat up all my pudding if you do go out."

"Thanks, Nana,"

Cass squeezed her grandma's hand. Nana patted her arm then left.

Cass sat up and pulled her cell phone out of her jeans pocket. She leaned back into the pillows on her bed and dialed another familiar number that Nana had inspired, instead.

"This is Norm."

"Hey, Norm, it's Cassidy French."

"Well hello there, Cass. How are you?"

"I'm hanging in there. Sorta. I wonder if we could meet to talk about my dad."

"Of course we can. I have court on Monday, how about Tuesday?"

"I was hoping something sooner. Like maybe now?"

He chuckled, but she didn't.

"Are you serious?"

"Yeah. I went to see him today, and I'm really upset about it. I'll even treat you to dinner. How's that?"

"Now, some of your grandma's cooking really would hit the spot."

"Oh, we can't meet here, I don't want to talk about this in front of my grandparents. Not yet."

"All right, then."

"What if we meet at Selby's. How soon could you meet me there?"

"Let me wrap up a couple of things here, then I could meet you in, say, an hour?"

"Perfect. See you then."

She ended the call, then rolled off the bed and onto her feet in one swift motion.

Chapter Ten

After a morning spent researching online Web site-building job services, and even placing an ad with one, Cass spent the next afternoon driving around to all of her Four-H kids for final checks and visits. At their dinner meeting the night before, Norm had given her a huge list of things to do if she was going to help stack the odds in her dad's favor for parole, and she decided to check on the progress of each of her kids' work before she got so busy that it slipped her mind.

Most of the kids participated because *they* wanted to, not because of any parental forcefulness, so she hardly ever had to chase after them to work on their projects. Usually her role involved making a suggestion or two about feed or about the animal's housing.

In the case of kids like Sally, she actually had to put the brakes on them before they took off into the stratosphere. Overachievers could be just as troublesome as underachievers, although she hadn't saved Sally for last because of her talent for being an overachiever. She had hoped to catch Mitch spending time with the family, but his truck wasn't in the yard when she pulled up.

"I'm glad you're here," Sally said as she and Cass walked back to the hog pen. "It's a crisis. His weight went up by half a pound. The last competition is in two weeks."

"That's hardly a crisis," Cass said. "He's still within his class, isn't he?"

"Yeah, but I don't want them to have any excuse to overlook him," Sally replied, heightened desperation in her voice. "Do you think I could give him a workout to do or something?"

"Something like *Sweatin' to the Piggies* instead of *Sweatin' to the Oldies*?"

"Perfect!"

Cass grinned and shook her head. "It doesn't work that way, sweetie."

"Well, what am I gonna do?"

Several pigs trotted over to their side of the pen and stuck their noses through the bars. Sally's made soft little grunt sounds between sniffs of them. Sally reached over and scratched him over his nose. He took her sleeve and nibbled on it.

“See. He eats *everything*,” Sally said with an exasperated sigh.

“You’re doing a great job with him, with all of them. I’m sure it’ll be fine.”

Sally didn’t look convinced. She bit her lip and studied him harder.

Cass kept quiet. This was part of the process, learning when to worry and when not to. Sally would probably drive herself nuts in the meantime, but she’d figure it out.

“So, how’s the rest of your family?” Cass asked, trying to be as subtle as she could.

Sally straightened and whirled around to look at Cass. “Did you really used to be my brother’s girlfriend?”

Cass blinked. So much for subtle.

“How did you find out about that?”

“Mom told me. We were in the kitchen rolling biscuits. I *love* rolling biscuits. And I thought maybe we could have you over to dinner, and Mitch could be there. ‘Cuz Mitch doesn’t have a girlfriend, and I don’t think you have a boyfriend. Do you?”

Cass shook her head. “No, I don’t have a boyfriend, and yes, I did used to be Mitch’s girlfriend, back when we were both in school.”

“But then you had a fight. Mom told me.”

Her tone was heavy and sad, then she blinked, and that energy bounced right back into her face and voice.

“But you’re not fighting anymore, right?”

"That's right."

"Okay, so, you can go back to being my brother's girlfriend."

"There you go with all your plans, again."

"I'm good at plans."

"So you want me to be part of your family? That's your plan?"

Sally nodded vigorously. "Then everything would be perfect."

Cass smiled. "I don't know about perfect, but I'll tell you a little secret. Mitch is coming over to my house tomorrow after church."

Sally's smile spread all over her face. "We have the same plan!"

"We have the same plan." Cass winked at Sally. "Just keep an eye on your pig here, and we'll see what Mother Nature has in store for both our plans. How's that?"

Sally nodded, and they both turned and walked back toward the house.

Cass didn't join her grandparents or any other First Baptist members for donuts and coffee after the Sunday morning sermon. She made a beeline for Brother Robert Sneed, minister of the church, who stood greeting members and visitors at the set of main doors at the rear of the sanctuary.

"Good morning, Brother Bob," Cass said, sticking her hand out for a good, old–fashioned shake.

He was somewhere between her father's age and Pop Pop's, although she'd never learned the exact number. His thin, dark hair had begun to gray at the temples, and his salt-and-pepper beard was more salt than pepper now.

"Cassidy French, what a pleasure to see you," he said, offering her a warm handshake and an even warmer smile. "I see you've been keeping your grandparents in line."

"They're pretty wily. It takes a firm hand."

They shared a grin.

"That reading that you gave. The one from Hebrews. That line about God casting our sins away and remembering them no more. Is that really true?"

"I believe it is."

"And it applies to all of us? Even if you break the law?"

He studied her a moment, then nodded. "It this about you or your father?"

She gave him a slight shrug. "Both, really."

"Well, it applies to both of you, I'm sure."

"I'm glad. I really liked that reading . . . and the things you said afterwards."

He gave her a patient, saintly nod, and she gathered up her courage for the next part.

"I was wondering if I could trouble you for a favor for my father. He has a parole hearing coming up, and his lawyer thinks if his minister could attend the hearing and speak on his behalf, then it might help his odds of getting paroled."

He didn't answer at first but stood there stroking his beard.

"Norm's been coaching me, helping me do all the things that need doing, so my dad qualifies for parole. Most of the time, people don't get it their first time, but he thinks if we do certain things, then he'll get it."

"And one of those things is to get a clergyman to speak on his behalf?"

Cass nodded. "You're a pillar of the community. And he'd be coming back to our community. The board would respect your input."

"Let me pray on it, and I'll talk to you later this week."

And suddenly, he was gone, moving around talking to church members, shaking hands, and offering more greetings.

"I was beginning to worry that you were going to stand me up," a familiar male voice said behind her.

She turned and held her breath as she took in the sight of Mitch in a navy suit with a solid olive-colored tie, and she really hoped the jade-colored sundress and white lace sweater she'd worn for the occasion had the same effect on him.

"I'd never do that."

They spent a moment in mutual appreciation of their Sunday's finest.

"You clean up nicely," she said with a smile.

"So do you." He returned the smile and took a step closer. "We're still on for tonight, right?"

"We sure are. I've been looking forward to it all week, especially after that visit with my dad."

"Your father wasn't happy to see you?"

She shook her head. "It wasn't that he wasn't happy to see me. It's just that he's"—she searched for the right words—"he's not himself. Not anymore. The longer he's in there, the worse he gets."

"I'm sorry to hear that. I had hoped he wouldn't be one of them, especially this close to release, or, possible release, rather."

"What do you mean, 'one of them?' "

Mitch let out a grim-sounding exhale. "Sometimes, on the inside, people turn. They don't just turn hard, like you see in movies where they become all violent. They turn within. They get lost. I read this article in a law enforcement magazine that talked about how over twenty-five percent of the prison population has moderate-to-severe depression. They get locked away, and they give up, even in the best of circumstances."

"Daddy can't be one of those. That can't happen to him."

Mitch put a hand on her shoulder. "Sometimes it can't be helped."

Cass bit her lower lip as the burden of worry settled over her, nearly bending her in two. Mitch's fingers clasped her shoulder in a reassuring squeeze, but it wasn't enough. She glanced over to Brother Sneed.

"He just has to help. He just has to."

Mitch turned in the same direction she was looking. "Who does?"

"Brother Sneed. I asked if he'd speak on my father's behalf at the parole hearing."

"That'd be great if he did. Who's idea was that?" Norm's?"

"Sort of. I mean, he told me to think of people who could speak on Daddy's side at the hearing, people who might have enough clout or a good enough argument to help sway the parole board in his favor. So he told me to think up as many people as I could and ask for their help."

"That's really smart, Cass," Mitch said, giving her another squeeze. "You're really determined to make this work, aren't you?"

"If that was all the family you had left, wouldn't you?"

He nodded. "Listen, tonight, we're just going to go out and have a nice time, just us, okay? I have to do one little errand for work, though, but it shouldn't take very long."

Cass frowned. "Can't it wait?"

He shook his head. "It's for work."

"You have to work tonight?"

"No, it's just something I volunteered to do really

quickly. It's not a big deal, won't even take us an hour."

She hated to disagree with him, but, yeah, it was a big deal. *Wait. Did he say us?*

"Not only do you expect to interrupt our date with work, but you expect me to help?"

He flashed her that secret-weapon smile, and her favorite dimple popped into view. She caved.

"I promise to make it as painless as possible. You might even enjoy it."

"All right. I'll see you at the house at suppertime, then."

He winked at her then headed toward the parking lot.

Nana and Cassidy putzed around the kitchen, putting the finishing touches on the dishes for Sunday supper while Pop Pop engaged in his after-church ritual of reading the paper. He always tucked himself away in his favorite recliner by the wood stove, a mug of coffee beside him on an end table, and Champ dozing contentedly at his feet.

"Who does that boy think he is?" Pop Pop boomed from the den.

Cassidy paused mid-napkin-fold and looked to Nana at the stove. The two women shared a grimace.

"What're you carryin' on about, Hank?"

Pop Pop stormed into the kitchen, the newspaper

in his hands. He turned the front page of the Living section around, so Nana and Cassidy could see it.

A single picture occupied most of the center of the page, a shot of Cass and her father in a hug as her father kissed the top of her head. Cass recognized it as their farewell at the end of Friday's visit.

But Ty had agreed to leave them. He promised he wouldn't take a picture.

"I thought you said he didn't take any pictures, he wasn't going to be all in our business like that," Pop Pop said, shaking the paper at Cass.

Cass threw her hands up. "He promised me he wouldn't. I don't even know how he got that picture. He left before Daddy even came in."

"I'm gonna drive down to the paper and tan that boy's hide," Pop Pop said, throwing the newspaper onto the dining table in disgust.

Cass picked it up.

"What's it say?" Nana asked.

Cass cleared her throat and read the caption beneath the photo. "Inmate Hank French Jr., convicted of killing his brother a decade ago, shares an emotional embrace with daughter Cassidy."

Nana gasped.

Cass clenched her teeth. She could only imagine what the article must say, if the caption was that bad.

How could Ty do this to them? He promised to draw attention to her family's plight. He said he'd draw attention to the upcoming parole hearing. He did *not* say he was going to crucify her father in the process. Where was the note that what he was convicted of was involuntary manslaughter, not first-degree murder?

And what was he doing using that picture? How did he even get it? He had no respect at all for the privacy she had requested for her family.

"I'll be right back, Nana," Cass said.

She left the kitchen and went to her apartment over the garage. She pulled out her cell phone and dialed Bethany.

Beth answered on the second ring.

"Ask me about my date last night. Go ahead. Ask me. Ty is awesome. We had the *best* time."

"Ty is a jerk, and if I see him again, I'm going to give him a piece of my mind. Pop Pop's ready to light torches and send a mob after him."

"What? Why?"

"Haven't you seen the paper today? Your *boyfriend* used a picture he did *not* have permission to take, and he wrote about my dad like he's a murderer, not a victim of circumstance."

"One date does not a boyfriend make, and, no, I haven't seen today's paper."

"Do you have plans with him today?"

"I'm not telling you if you're going to ask like that. You sound like a crazy person."

"Tell you what, just go read the paper, then see how crazy you think I am. I have to go."

Cass closed the phone and paced around her bedroom.

Cecil walked in silently then jumped onto the bed. He meowed at her insistently.

"So, do you have some complaint too?"

He replied with another round of mewing. He seemed to be looking behind her, so she glanced over her shoulder.

The shade was still drawn over the window. Cecil didn't have his square of sunlight to sleep in with the shade down.

"All right, boy."

Cass turned, then reached over and pulled up the shade. Sunlight covered the bottom half of the bed. Cecil immediately walked over to it, walked around in a circle, then he plopped down in the center of the light.

"I'm glad somebody's day just got better."

Cecil rolled onto his back and reached out one paw at her.

Cass used her index finger to scratch his forehead, directly between his ears, and she could hear his purr as clearly as if she'd bent her head down to his level.

The sound of a truck pulling up the drive turned her attention to the yard, and she looked out the window.

Mitch's truck eased to a stop beside the farmhouse.

Cass sighed. She'd been looking forward to her date with Mitch for days. So had her grandma. But the mood had definitely been spoiled around the French farm within the past ten minutes.

Cass flipped open her cell phone and paged through the numbers until she found Ty's. She hit send.

She tapped her foot while she waited to see if he would answer his phone or if she'd get dumped into voicemail. She got the second option.

When the beep sounded, she said very clearly, "Ty Thomas. Just saw your article. You are a complete jerk, and if I *never* see you again, it'll be too soon."

She ended the call, turned off her phone, and went down to meet Mitch and to start a date that was *long* overdue.

Unfortunately, the pall of anger and frustration that hung over the dinner table squelched everyone's appetite, and the clean-up afterwards held slightly more warmth than a wake.

So when Mitch reminded Cass that he needed to run his errand for work and asked if she'd like to go for a drive, she dragged him to the door the second the question was out of his mouth.

"The timing for this couldn't be more perfect," Mitch said once they were in his truck and on their way through town.

"You can say that again. I know one reporter who better steer clear of Cumberland Springs for a while."

Mitch grinned, then he flashed her a more serious look. "You have to promise me one thing."

"Um, okay."

Cass wasn't sure what to make of his expression.

"For the rest of the night, no talking about Ty or his article or your dad or his parole hearing. Deal?"

Words of protest gathered on the tip of her tongue, but she held them back. It's not like she would shrivel up and die if she just *had* to sit here and bask in the warmth of Mitch's company for a couple hours.

"All right. You have a deal."

Chapter Eleven

Cumberland Springs received its name from two different factors. The first was its positioning along the Cumberland Plateau, a wide, flat tableau of land several counties in length and broken only by the occasional dots of rolling Tennessee hills. It contained some of the best farmland this side of the Mississippi Delta.

The other factor was the collection of natural springs on the west side of the town. The residents had rallied together to build a large park and recreational facility around them, and they were the biggest, brightest jewel in the town's crown.

Only one road led to the Cumberland Springs Park, so as soon as Mitch turned the pickup down Springs Drive, Cass knew where he was headed.

"Why, Mitchell Riley, what are you up to?"

Mitch just whistled an innocent little tune and pointed toward the top of the windshield.

"Are those stars up there? Look at that."

Cass snickered, but she turned her eyes toward the sky anyway. Nothing inspired awe like the country sky at night.

When she was younger, her dad used to celebrate special occasions with her by grabbing two sleeping bags and taking her for a campout somewhere on the farm. They'd lie under the stars and listen to the sounds of crickets, the lowing of the cattle, all those wonderful sounds that, to her, meant everything was right with the world.

Mitch stopped the truck in front of the gateway leading into the park. The large, metal, yellow bar was down and blocked the drive.

He put the truck in park and got out. Cass sat up straighter and watched him. He strutted up to the bar, unlocked the chain, and pushed it back to its holding place during the park's normal operating hours.

He came back to the truck, put it in drive, moved forward several feet, then put it in park again.

"Are you breaking into the park?"

"I plead the fifth."

He got out and replaced the bar across the driveway.

When he climbed back into the truck, he turned to her and said, "And no, I'm not breaking into the park. The ranger thinks there might be people sneaking in here at night, after hours, so we come in here from time to time to check things out, give him a hand."

Mitch drove into parking lot A and pulled the truck into the first space and turned off the engine. He reached beneath his seat and dug out a large black flashlight. He opened the driver door and got out of the truck. Cass unbuckled the seat belt and opened her own door then climbed down.

"We'll just poke around the most likely areas," he said.

He motioned for her to stand just a little behind him. She smiled and complied, more than happy to let him play modern-day knight, if that's what he wanted.

They walked past the open area where the springs were located. A series of concrete walkways and platforms extended around and connected each of the springs. They looked like a series of misshapen hot tubs or whirlpools. All of them were round, but each one had a slightly different shape and size to it.

Cass' favorite was one of the smaller ones that resembled a kidney bean. The pools of water held smaller silver reflections of the half-moon and the stars. Those shimmers, along with the halo of Mitch's flashlight, were the only accompaniment to the glow of the night sky.

Mitch checked out the men's restroom first, then they quietly moved to the opposite side of the building to examine the women's.

He led her toward the picnic pavilions, but she didn't move as quickly as he did in the dark. He probably had a lot more experience at this kind of thing.

She stumbled and barely managed to keep herself upright.

"Psst," she whispered, and he stopped.

"What?" he whispered back.

"I can't go that fast. Give me your hand."

She felt around in the air where she guessed his hand would be. She slipped her hand into his warm, firm, grip and instantly felt steadied.

Step by step, they made their way around the most popular sections of the park, without finding any signs of disturbance or occupation.

"That should do it," Mitch announced, leading her across the open, grassy fields, back toward the springs.

Cass had no idea how much time the tour had taken them, but she could have walked across the entire state with her hand in his like that.

"Okay, now that the work is done . . ." Mitch said, giving her hand a little squeeze as they arrived back at the springs.

He waved at the series of shimmering pools before them. "Take your pick."

Cass looked from spring to spring. "What do you mean? I didn't know to bring my suit."

Did Mitch have some sort of late-night skinny dip in mind? Beth would flip when Cass told her. She always said it was the quiet ones who came up with the most scandalous adventures.

"Guess you're just going to have to throw a little trust my way," Mitch said in such a deliciously husky voice, Cass had to force herself to concentrate and not swoon.

Mitch took a step closer to her. He reached around her, and she felt him lift the bulk of her braid. With a gentle tug, he pulled off the rubber band, and his fingers wove through her hair, releasing each layer of braiding.

Every corner of her body exploded with a flood of life and awareness that she hadn't felt in so long that she thought she'd forgotten how. She closed her eyes, and in that moment, she became sixteen again, standing in the moonlight with a boy for the first time ever.

Suddenly, she was aware of infinite sensations all scrambling through her and competing for her attention.

Passion, of course, took center stage. Next came a wave of calm and familiarity that warmed her like a big, fluffy comforter. They'd been one another's first and—if Beth's assessments were correct—only loves.

Everything they'd learned about love and a lot about life, had been with one another. You couldn't put a price tag on that kind of intimacy. You could scarcely put any type of label on it. It was like suddenly finding an old pair of jeans you thought you'd given to charity. Not only were they still there, but when you slipped them on, they felt even better than before.

Lastly there was one sensation that had been gone so long she'd forgotten all about it, hope. Standing next to Mitch like this, feeling the nearness of him, the sureness of him, she could have sworn that anything was possible.

Even as cruel as life and fate had proven that they could be, his presence vanquished them with the prowess of any knight of legend. Standing with him, just the two of them in the moonlight, with the soft chirp of crickets as accompaniment, well, she didn't just feel like good things were possible, they were now probable.

The smell of his cologne, the feel of his hands in her hair, the soft and sure burbles of water in time to their rhythmic breathing—all of it filled her with a mixture of so much hope and security. Suddenly, she was invincible.

Every single one of these thoughts and feelings came to her as his sure, steady hands combed through her hair. He didn't stop until he had freed each and every strand.

When she felt the back of his fingers touch her temple, she opened her eyes. That emerald gaze of his held such a potent combination of intensity and awe that she almost faltered beneath the weight of it. But his touch gave her strength.

He drew his fingers down the side of her face with a touch so tender and light, it was like a whisper on her skin.

She tipped her head up, turning her face more toward his. If he didn't kiss her now, she'd explode.

"Not yet," he whispered, and his breath danced across her lips.

He put a hand on each of her hips then knelt in front of her.

"What are you doing?" she asked. "Besides driving me absolutely mad, I mean."

He looked up at her. A boyish grin lit up his whole face, and she swayed on her feet.

"The perfect arrest requires a slow, careful stakeout. You can't rush it. You can't skip any steps."

He drew his hand along the outside of her left thigh and around to the back of her calf, all the way down to the hem of her jeans.

"If you don't do it by the book, then your target gets away from you, and it's gone forever."

She had to put her hand down to steady herself against his shoulder.

"Are you trying to arrest me?" she asked with barely enough voice behind the words to be heard over the springs.

He tugged backward on the hem until, like a horse being shod, she raised her foot up off the ground.

He looked up at her. "If I have my way, you'll be in my custody forever."

She melted and had to put her other hand on his other shoulder to hold herself perfectly still. She didn't want to miss a second of whatever he had in mind next.

He slipped her left shoe off, then he guided her bare foot back down to the ground. The soft, springy grass cushioned her foot, and she wiggled her toes against it.

He repeated the process with her right foot. Then he did something she totally didn't expect. With slow, deliberate fingers, he rolled up each pants leg in turn, all the way up past her knees.

When he finished, he stood once more then took her left hand in his right. He led her to the edge of the egg-shaped spring.

"Have a seat," he said.

She sat down while he kicked off his boots a few feet beside her. She leaned over and swatted the top of his foot.

"What was that for?" he asked.

"If you think you're going to do all that for me, then you're just gonna stand over there and steal my thunder, you're sadly mistaken."

He chuckled, and she reached for the bottom of his jeans, tugging a few times until he moved closer. She started with his right leg, rolling the denim up again and again until she had it in a small, tight cuff. She had to use both hands to work it up over the hard, well-muscled lines of his calf, but, at last, she got it into place up and over his knee.

She did the same for his left leg, but slower this time. Once she had the denim above his knee, she gave the back of his knee a quick pinch then scraped her fingernails down the back of his leg.

He actually made a yipping sound, but when she tried to do it again, he jumped away from her. She rolled to the side and onto her feet, then she chased after him, bending low to the ground and holding her hands out like a crab's pincers.

He stopped a few feet away and stood his ground. "That's not funny."

"Hard to take that as an authoritative answer when you were just shrieking like a girl a second ago."

"I mean it. You better stop that."

She took another step forward, and, faster than she ever would have believed, he dipped down, charged at her, and caught her midsection against his shoulder. He straightened, lifting her off the ground, and she squealed.

Giggling wildly, she squirmed, but his solid grip didn't waver for even an instant. He walked her back to the spring, and jostled her.

"You're going to stop, right? I'd hate to have to drop you into the spring."

"Okay, okay," she managed to say between giggles.

He set her down, and she straightened to face him. Between their playing and the shimmers coming off the water, his face glowed within its silver halo. She placed an open palm on each side of his face, cupping it and guiding him forward.

He moved with her until they were nose to nose. At the same moment, each of them titled their heads, and their lips finally met. The kiss was so tender, she almost cried. Once, twice, even a third time, their mouths came together, and Cass was stunned she could remain on her feet.

They paused for a breath, and their eyes opened as if on an unspoken cue. They stood there, their gazes mingling, their breaths mingling. He touched his nose to hers once more, and they burst into laughter at the light, tickling touch.

"I swear, Cass, you make me feel like a kid again. I bet I could do just about anything in the world right now."

"Me, too," she said, and smiled as she moved her hands down each side of his face. His skin was soft and smooth and without stubble.

"C'mere," he said, pulling her down with him to the side of the spring. They scooted to the very edge of the concrete and dipped their feet into the water. Soothing warmth rushed up her legs, massaging and caressing her skin. Mitch wrapped his left arm around her shoulders and reeled her in even closer.

Her natural instinct was to lean her head against his chest, and she didn't fight it. She touched her forehead to the place where his collarbone was. He kissed the top of her head.

She wiggled her toes and swung her legs back and forth, swirling the water. She could feel similar movements from Mitch's direction.

They sat in perfect silence like that for a long while. For that time, nothing else was of any consequence. They were the only people in their little world.

The rest of the evening had been perfectly delightful, and not mentioning Ty or his evil article or even her worries about her dad had been easy.

Far too soon, Mitch was pulling into the driveway of the farm. Cass hardly wanted to say good night, but as things were, she was going to have a pretty tough time dragging herself out of bed in the morning.

Cass unbuckled her seat belt.

"I was thinking about your dad," Mitch said as he put the truck in park then turned off the engine. "What if I speak out for him too?"

Cass gasped. What a wonderful idea.

"Would you do that? That would be fantastic!"

"Of course I'll help you and your dad."

Cass leaned over and threw her arms around Mitch. "You're the best."

She relaxed the hug, but she didn't move away. They remained like that for quite some time. Their arms locked in a loving embrace. Their eyes devoured one another with emotions that had been imprisoned for years, but rather than waste away, they had grown and intensified.

So many feelings whirled like a Texas twister in a clear path from Cass' head to her heart. Love. There was no other word for it. The feeling hadn't disappeared. It hadn't died.

Not only was her love for Mitch alive and well, but it threatened to jump out of her chest and tell him if she didn't find a way to do it herself.

"Mitch," Cass began, her gaze never wavering for his.

"I have to ask a favor," he said at the same time.

"Anything."

"Be my date to the fair Saturday?" And the dance after? Once your judging is done, that is."

She nodded. "You got it."

He hugged her again, much more tightly than a simple yes to a date request deserved.

"I've missed you so much," Mitch interjected.

He held on so tightly, Cass couldn't imagine how they'd ever come apart again.

Chapter Twelve

Cassidy felt like she had just closed her eyes when the rooster crowed. She pulled the covers up over her head. What a shame roosters didn't come with snooze buttons.

Cass moved through the morning chores pretty easily, once she was up. Moving through Nana's maze of questions about her date proved more difficult.

As an afterthought, she came back to her apartment and checked her e-mail. It'd been a couple of days since she placed her ad about her Web skills, and she might have a message or two.

She gasped when she saw her inbox. Eighty-seven messages. Holy cow!

How in the world could she have so many messages already? It wasn't like she was the only coder in the world. She hadn't even been the only coder advertising with that site. Maybe she hadn't priced herself correctly?

Could there really be that many companies out there that needed help?

Cass backed away from the computer and went downstairs to pull a can of Mountain Dew from the fridge. She definitely needed a caffeine infusion before she tackled that list.

Two hours and three sodas later, she'd whittled the list down to half a dozen jobs she could manage by their deadlines.

Turning down so much work put a knot in her stomach. Goodness knows she needed the money for the farm, but she still had several people to ask to help her dad, and there just weren't enough hours in the day to do it all.

She'd just finished the third page for her first client when her cell phone rang.

"Hello?"

"Cassidy, it's Norm Greer."

"Oh, hi, Norm."

"I spent the morning with your dad, and I finally talked him into seeing the doctor. Looks like he has bronchitis."

"That can't be good."

"Well, it's not, but I think this might actually play in our favor. The longer he's in there, the worse it's going to get for him, and we have one of the best cases I've ever seen for proving that he can become a contributing member of the community instead of continuing to be a drain on it."

"What about . . . you know, the psych stuff, the depression stuff?"

"I'm still working on that. It's more complicated than something obvious like a cough. I'm on it, though. What about the character witnesses?"

"Brother Sneed said he needed to think about it. He told me we'd talk later this week, but he hasn't called yet. I was thinking about dropping by his office. The good news is I have an extra one. Mitch Riley has agreed to testify on his behalf."

"Someone from the sheriff's department? That's a great start. Brother Sneed would be a great follow-up. One or two more, and we should have a fail-proof lineup."

"I'm doing everything I can. Is my dad going to be okay, though? How bad is his infection?"

"They've got him on medication, and I asked the doctor to see if he couldn't officially reduce his workload for a week or so. Give your dad a chance to heal and rest. They're going to do what they can."

"I know my grandparents say this to you all the time, but I'm going to say it too. Thanks for everything, Norm."

"You got it, Cassidy. But it's still third and long for us. We've got one more down to go. I'll swap more notes with you later."

"Sure thing."

She hung up the phone and hoped that Norm knew the law as well as he knew football. It was her father's only hope. She grabbed her truck keys and headed for the church.

Cassidy paused before the open doorway to Brother Sneed's office. He had a typical minister's office—shelves full of books with scholarly dissections of significant people or events from the *Bible*, framed diplomas on the walls, a family portrait of himself, his wife, and both daughters. Two mismatched armchairs sat opposite his desk, evidence that the décor relied on donations from a budget-stretched membership and not an established fund from a national office.

Brother Sneed didn't have a name plaque on his desk or his door. What Cassidy's eyes settled on immediately was the thick wooden block carved into the shape of an alligator. Holes had been drilled into the top of it, deep enough for it to hold pens and pencils. It had been hand-painted by Bitsy Sneed in the same Vacation Bible School class where Cassidy had painted one for Nana and Pop. They, too, still had theirs on display by the phone in the kitchen.

Brother Sneed hadn't looked up from his reading, so Cass knocked on the door.

"Hello, Cassidy. Come in."

He stood and waved to the chairs, donning his

most benevolent smile as he waited for her to choose one. She took the seat closest to the door, and once she settled in it, he sat down again.

"What brings you in today?"

"Well, I was hoping you'd be able to tell me whether you can help my father, if you can make it to his parole hearing."

The benevolence disappeared. Something akin to discomfort replaced it. He leaned back into his chair and stroked his Moses-like beard. Cass suspected he grew the thing just so he could stroke it sagely in moments such as these.

"Here's the thing. I've discussed it with some of the elders, and we're not sure if this is the best time to take on an endeavor of this nature."

"An endeavor of what nature? Supporting a member of your flock in need of forgiveness and understanding?"

"There's more to it than that, Cassidy. This kind of support, this kind of event, well, it has some political connotations that not all of our members are comfortable endorsing."

"Political connotations? This has nothing to do with politics. This has to do with atonement and forgiveness. This is about healing a family, healing a community. The only endorsement you're sending is that God's love and forgiveness apply to all repentant hearts."

"That's your point of view because this is *your*

family we're talking about, Cassidy. I think if you had the ability to step back and see the bigger picture, you'd have a greater appreciation for just how sensitive a matter like this can be. The *Bible* is very clear on matters of punishment as well as forgiveness."

The only thing that kept her from rolling her eyes at him was the knowledge that Nana would probably give herself a herniated disc trying to turn Cass over her knee for disrespecting an elder. She dug her thumbnail into the seam of the armchair's padding.

"Let me get this straight. There are people here who think my father deserves to stay locked up in that prison and left to rot? There are people here who, despite hearing you preach about love and forgiveness, think that those things don't apply to a man like my father, so they're trying to forbid you from participating?"

Brother Sneed stroked his beard, and Cass knew better than to push for a concrete answer.

To think, she'd taken a break she couldn't really afford from her coding to push for help from a man who cared more about perception than truth, who chose the easy thing over the right thing.

She stood up. "Well, I thank you for your time. I just wish you really meant those words you said, about love and forgiveness and sins being remembered no more. You'd think that if our family could make peace with this, everyone else could too."

She turned and walked out of the office.

"Cassidy, wait."

"Not this time," she called over her shoulder. "I'm done waiting."

The very last livestock fair of the season always brought one of the biggest social events of the year to Cumberland Springs: The Pig Ball.

Even though farmers never really had an offseason, the Pig Ball gave the farmers and townsfolk alike an end-of-the-year blowout to celebrate the completion of their busiest time of year.

Daytime festivities included a parade and hayride through the town, featuring various local celebrities such as the mayor, the winners of both the livestock and the baking events, and so forth, then it concluded with a dance beneath the stars at the Cumberland Springs park pavilion.

Cass was determined to have a new dress for it, even if her Four-H schedule meant she had to change into it in a horse stall.

And of course where there was shopping, there was Bethany. She'd managed to finagle an afternoon off so they could drive into Nashville and find just the right outfits for the special occasion.

The hour-long drive into Music City felt like it flew by in minutes with all the talking Cass and Beth had to do. Plus, they were cranking Shania in the primo sound system Bethany had splurged on when she bought her little hybrid. Shania always put some pep into any drive.

Once Bethany actually saw the paper and read Ty's caption and article, she had a greater appreciation for Cass' feelings about one Ty Thomas.

"It's a shame Tyler's so cute, because he sure did turn out to be rotten to the core. He practically called your father a murderer. If I were you, I'd punch him next time I saw him. I might just punch him for ya."

"You're a real pal." Cass shot her friend a smile. "But if a punch is all he gets, he'll be the luckiest man in Cumberland Springs. I thought Pop Pop was gonna get the shotgun off the wall after her saw the paper."

"I have to say, I may envy you for the good guy mojo you've got going on with Mitch, but I do *not* envy all this garbage you're going through with your dad."

Cass wasn't sure what to say to that. At least she had a dad.

"You know you'd do the same if it were your father," Cass finally replied.

"Yeah, but I'd go grey in the process."

Cass reached for another carrot stick. They had decided on healthy snacks today, because as all women knew, eating right the day you go to try on new clothes somehow magically undid any wrong eating you'd done in the weeks prior.

"I'd probably have a little easier time of it if Ty hadn't printed what he printed."

"I can't believe he turned out to be such a snake."

"You never can tell with folks anymore."

"He keeps calling me too. You'd think he'd figure out I'm not going out with him again, no matter how cute he is. I'm telling you, it's time to pass around the collection plate and buy that boy a clue."

Cass laughed and munched on the sweet, juicy carrot. Her cell phone rang, and she pulled it from her jean pocket. She glanced at the number but didn't recognize it. As she flipped it open to take the call, Beth reached over and turned down the radio for her.

"This is Cassidy."

"Yes, I'm trying to reach Cassidy French," a man's voice stated politely.

"You've got her."

"I'm Ben Rhodes, and I'm calling on behalf of Echo Enterprises in Nashville. We responded to your ad because we were looking for a Web designer, but you said you weren't able to take the job."

"Yeah, I'm really sorry about that. I got many more offers than I could fill by their deadlines. I just thought it would be more fair if I declined so you could find someone else who could meet your deadline."

"We appreciate the consideration, of course, but we have a pretty unique situation, and we're actually quite desperate, especially since your credentials list the two coding languages we use the most."

"Oh? I didn't realize that was unique."

That might explain why she had such an influx of work requests.

"In light of the situation, we're actually prepared to triple your price, provided you can deliver the Web site within a week."

Cass almost dropped the phone. *Triple?*

"That's very generous, but I do still have clients I was able to accept work from, and I do owe them their work."

"If you're looking to negotiate for more money, I can go a little higher, but, we're pretty close to the ceiling for this project."

"I'm not trying to ask for more money. I just need you to understand, that I have to do the right thing by the clients I've already accepted."

"Okay. We can go a little higher. How about another five percent?"

Cass pulled the phone away from her ear and looked at it. Did he not understand that not everything could be bought?

She thought about his offer. Originally, she had accepted only enough jobs as she could fit into a normal workday and that could be worked around her farm chores and coaching responsibilities.

This was the final week and the final livestock show of the year, and if she took this job, she'd have *no* free time and might even have to shirk her chores.

And what about the people she needed to talk to about her dad's parole hearing?

But triple the fee she had requested? That could easily pay two months of bills for the entire farm and then some.

Opportunities like that didn't just crop up every day. She couldn't turn her back on that, either. She put the phone back to her ear.

"Look, Mr. Rhodes, this isn't just about money. By accepting those jobs, I have to deliver. I'm willing to see if I can help you but—"

"Would you be willing to come to our offices downtown to talk this over?"

"Downtown Nashville?"

"If that's a problem, I can come to you."

"It's not a problem. As luck would have it, I am actually on my way into Nashville today. I might be able to meet with you."

Cass glanced over at Bethany and shrugged at her to see if this was okay. Beth nodded.

"Great. When can you be here?"

Cass pulled a napkin and pen from the glove box.

"Give me the directions, I can be there in half an hour, depending on traffic."

She jotted down the directions then ended the call.

"Talk about pushy," she said as she re-capped her pen.

"What was that all about?"

"That ad I put out, offering to do people's Web sites? I don't know what I did or said that was so right in it, but I'm being hammered with work requests. And this guy just offered me triple my fee if I'll get his done within the week."

"I don't know what your fee is, but triple anything sounds like a sweet deal."

"Yeah, if I don't mind not sleeping for seven days. I already took on a few other jobs, and I can't dump all my chores for an entire week. Add to that, I still need to round up a few more people to testify on my dad's behalf."

"Shouldn't Norm be helping more with that?"

"He thought the request would pack more of a punch coming from me versus him."

"Is there something I can do to help?"

"Besides learn to code in two hours or less? Not really. Thanks, though. Just drop me off at this meeting, let me get the specs, then we can go home."

"No dress?"

"I'm not going to be able to go to the Pig Ball if I take this job."

"You *have* to go to the Pig Ball. You've worked as hard as anyone else this season. Plus, all your kids and their parents will be there."

"I don't see how."

"Look, just hit this meeting and find out what's involved. Maybe it won't be as bad as you're afraid it will be."

Cass stared at the road ahead and hoped that was true.

"It's not quite as bad as I feared, but it's pretty bad," Cass announced as she climbed back into Beth's Prius over two hours later.

"Am I even going to understand what you're about to say, or is this going to be more techno-babble-geekazoid computer language?"

Cass buckled her seat belt. "Both. The good news is that their images have already been created, so re-sizing is all I'll have to do on that, and that's simple. Most of the text is ready, and what's not ready will be within a day or two. The hard part will be the on-line forms they need me to build. Those things take forever."

"Do you think you can do it?"

"With everything else on my plate? Sure, if I put in an IV drip of Red Bull, stop sleeping, and clone myself."

"So, you said no?" Beth asked as she eased into the traffic and started them on their way home.

Cass sighed. "Call me crazy, but I said yes."

"I've known you my whole life. I have dozens of legitimate reasons to call you crazy."

Cass didn't even crack a smile at the joke. "Seriously, I have too many chances to do good things for my family right now. Daddy's hearing and this money for the farm, they were just too good to pass up."

"I'll remind you that you said that when you start snapping at people for changing the channel too loudly."

Cass groaned at the mention of one of her's and Beth's only childhood fights, an argument over Beth's remote control after a sleepover that involved all talk and no sleep for either of them.

"I'm going to have to give up something, though. Besides just a few hours of sleep. I'm going to have to back out of the ball."

"You can't do that. You have to go to the ball."

"It's the easiest thing to give up. The judging will be over, and Mitch will understand when I tell him about this job and the money it will mean."

"Just trust me. You really have to go."

What wasn't Beth telling her? Did she know something that was going to happen at the ball? Had some one seen Mitch out buying an engagement ring or something? Beth wasn't quite as well connected to the Cumberland Spring as Nana, but she was pretty close.

"Why?"

"I can't tell you."

"Which, of course, means you *have* to tell me."

"No, I don't."

On they went for the rest of the ride home, with Cass threatening all sorts of retribution, and Beth refusing to crack. When threats didn't work, Cass tried her best bribery, and still, her best friend wouldn't come clean.

"Fine, I'm never speaking to you again," Cass said as they pulled into driveway to the farm.

"Now I *know* you don't mean that," Beth said then blew a raspberry. "Besides, I can tell you now. But first we have to go to the trunk."

Cass frowned. No way did Beth have Mitch in her trunk. So maybe this wasn't about Mitch at all?

They went around to the back.

"I had to make sure you wouldn't throw some kind of fit and make me turn around."

"Why would I make you turn around?"

Bethany opened the trunk. Inside were several shopping bags and two long, black, zippered sheaths with Montgomery Dress Shoppe embroidered on them.

Cass looked at her friend with an unspoken question in her eyes. The only things that came from that place were wedding dresses, but there's no way that was what was inside those casings.

"You better like this, or I'm divorcing you," Beth said, lifting the top bag.

"What? Why? When?" Cass couldn't even get a full question out.

"I had to do something while you were in that meeting. I had already decided I was going to get my dress for the Pig Ball, so I headed for the mall, but on my way, I saw this big clearance banner at Montgomery's. Now that all the summer weddings are over, they've got loads of bridesmaids dresses on sale.

Well, wedding dresses, too, but I'd say that's a little premature."

Cass forced herself to laugh, especially since she'd just been silly enough to entertain the thought that a proposal might be in the works.

She unzipped the bag and gold shimmers of light sparkled inside the opening. She pulled the dress out. It was a simple strapless, knee-length dress, but it was made of a gold shimmering fabric so beautiful that Cass was almost afraid to touch it.

"It's gorgeous!" Cass exclaimed.

"Isn't it? So now you have to go. Just for an hour. You don't even have to get yourself ready. I can come over and do your hair while you sit at the computer. I mean, I'm not going to dress you, but I'll do everything I can."

Cass reached over and hugged Beth.

"You are the best. You are the absolute best friend a girl could ever have."

"You've been there for me plenty."

Beth put the dress back in its sheath, gave it to Cass then handed her another white plastic bag.

"Pantyhose and other goodies in here."

"Let me see yours."

Beth showed off hers with equal pride. It was an aqua-colored dress with a halter–style bodice.

Cass wolf-whistled her approval.

"Now, you just take care of getting all that computer junk done."

Cass kept staring at the bags. Even on clearance, those dresses were still probably in the triple digits. She hugged her friend again.

"I can't thank you enough for this. At least let me pay you back for my dress."

"We'll talk about it when that big, whopper check of yours shows up."

Beth put her dress back and closed the trunk. "Now, get going. I can't do *everything* myself."

Cass gave her a third, quick hug then took off for her loft apartment.

Nana and Pop Pop hadn't understood how Cass had gotten so much work, and they sure didn't understand it when she tried to explain the type of work she had to do. In the end, the best she could do was ask them to trust her and to give her a week. Then, she buckled down for the biggest batch of code-crunching she'd done since college.

Despite Cass' best attempts to exist on a liquid diet of Mountain Dew and whatever energy drinks she'd been able to snag from the Quick Stop convenience store, Nana made sure to bring her a hot breakfast and an afternoon snack. Guilt drove Cass to the dinner table at the end of the day where she would watch her grandparents' eyes glaze over when she tried to explain the progress she'd made.

Just before bedtime each night, Pop Pop would sneak up to leave a Little Debbie Zebra Cake on the corner of her desk. Then, as always, he'd pull a quarter out of her ear.

After four days of that, Cass didn't have a word for what she felt, but she was pretty sure it would be a new entry in the definition of exhausted. She hit the sheets Friday night ready for the break that Saturday's judging and festivities would bring.

The last thing Cass could claim to be the next morning was mentally sharp.

"Hey, where are you going, kid?" Pop Pop asked sharply from the passenger seat.

"What?" Cass asked, suddenly aware that they had passed right by the entrance to the fairgrounds.

"Oh for crying out loud," she said, saving him the trouble of chastising her.

She turned around at the first decent spot she could and headed back to the entrance.

"Sorry, Pop Pop. I'm not firing on all cylinders today."

"I sure am. Old Man Simpson's in for the battle of his life today. My chili's gonna send 'em all cryin' back to their mamas!"

Cass could have used a chili infusion just to help wake her up. Mountain Dew didn't cut it anymore, and she had already cleared the Quick Stop out of Red Bull.

She had no clue how she'd make it to the Pig Ball tonight.

The morning passed with the rabbit, poultry, and lamb competitions and not a single one of her kids earned ribbons. Her funk must have been contagious.

She made her way to the line for Charmaine's Chicken Shack. Some broasted chicken over a salad might re-spark some of her energy.

Her mind was still on her kids and the afternoon ahead when she noticed movement behind her. More people desperate for Charmaine's magic chicken, no doubt.

If luck was on her side, the judging would move quickly this afternoon. She'd give all of her kids the night and time for their end-of-the-year dinner at Selby's, then she'd rush home to change for the Pig Ball.

If luck was *really* on her side, she'd even have time for a quick nap, so she could greet Mitch with the ready-for-a-night-on-the-town expression she wanted to greet him with, as opposed to the too-pooped-to-party expression she felt.

"There's the little lady right now. Hey, Cassidy, want to hear what your voicemail sounds like on my end?"

Cass turned around slowly, afraid that the face she would find behind her actually matched the voice she had never wanted to hear again.

Behind her stood Ty and another man with a brown canvas photographer's bag hanging from his shoulder.

Ty's expression held a mixture of victory and cockiness that sent annoyance burrowing along her spine until it reached the center of her forehead and nested into a throbbing goose egg of pure irritation.

The other man simply held her in a gaze filled with amusement. Both men looked so smug, she wanted to smack them.

Ty looked to the other man and put the phone between them as the message played.

Ty laughed. "I love that part about 'If I never see you again, it'll be too soon.' Guess now is never, huh, Miss Cassidy French."

Cass charged between the two men like a defensive lineman, batting at Ty's phone in the process. Both men grunted as she pushed past, and Ty's phone clattered against the ground.

"Creep," she added over her shoulder.

She didn't have time to spar with Ty, verbally or otherwise. And that push was all of her energy that he was going to get. She was too tired and too frazzled. Her schedule was packed tighter than ten pounds of garbage in a five pound sack, and she didn't want to waste another moment on him.

She headed back to the livestock area and hoped one of the many club parents was around and willing—as they often were—to grab lunch or share theirs. She was almost back to the pavilion when shouting nearby finally permeated the fog of irritation surrounding her.

"You're goin' down this time, Riley!"

She turned around and sought the source of the voice. They were beside the "Dunk a Cop/Dunk the DA" booth, and there, suspended on a wooden plank over a tank of water, sat Mitch. He had on faded blue jeans and an orange T-shirt, and he wore a baseball cap with the logo for the sheriff's department.

"I'll take three," Wes Tucker said as he plopped his money down in front of the vendor.

"Might as well give him the whole bucket," Mitch called. "He couldn't hit the broad side of a barn."

Cass walked over to the side of the tank away from the target. She put a hand up over her eyes to shield them from the sun, then looked up at Mitch.

"How'd you get roped into this?" she asked.

"I volunteered for an early shift. I wanted to get it over with, plus, it freed me up to take some girl to the Pig Ball."

"Lucky girl."

"Hey, I'm feeling lucky today too. I've been here almost an hour, and no one's dunked me yet."

"Oh we can't have that," she said, then turned and lined up behind Wes.

"If he doesn't get you, I will," she said loudly enough to get Mitch's attention.

He shot her his most disarming grin, and the sight of that Riley dimple made her heart flutter.

"You wouldn't do that to me, would you?"

A loud clang interrupted their flirt-filled gazes. Wes' first ball had missed the target and slammed into the cage above Mitch.

"Oh c'mon, you can do better than that," Cass said encouragingly.

"Hey, who's side are you on?" Mitch asked.

The next ball whizzed through the air and clipped the top of the metal arm holding the target. The ball shot up into the air then spun away behind the tank.

"Told ya," Mitch said.

Wes grunted as he made his final throw. No metallic clang sounded this time. The ball whizzed by the target by mere inches and thudded into the hay bales behind it.

Mitch howled with laughter while Wes grumbled under his breath. He gave Mitch a dismissive wave and marched off, still muttering to himself.

Cass put her hands on her hips and regarded Mitch for a long time. She loved the way he looked with the sun highlighting the brown waves of his hair and laughter lighting his entire face.

She had just decided to leave him high and dry when a most unwelcome voice haunted her once more.

"I'll take a shot at this game," Ty said from behind her. "Who could pass up a chance to knock Mitch Riley off his pedestal?"

She whirled around, and there he stood again, the photographer at his side. Both of them had their hands full with Charmaine's chicken baskets, so neither one had their money out yet.

"Oh no you don't," Cass said, shoving her hand into her front pocket. She slapped a twenty dollar bill in front of the vendor. "I'm buying the whole bucket. I want every ball you have."

The freckly faced teenage boy looked at her with eyes wide and reached for the bill as though he were afraid it might bite him or something.

"Here, I've got twenty-five for you," Ty said.

He stepped forward and put his food basket down on the counter.

"Forty bucks for the bucket," Cass said, digging into her backup stash of cash in her left pocket.

She dropped the money on top of her original twenty, then she vaulted over the counter, barely missing Ty's food. He scrambled to move it out of the way as she passed. When she landed on the opposite side, she bent over and snatched up the metal bucket full of balls.

The photographer started laughing, but Ty stood there and just stared at her.

"Fine," he said. "Start throwing."

She put the bucket on the ground, then sat on it like a hen on a pile of eggs. She folded her arms across her chest and shot him a look that just dared him to try to come and take one.

"Get on out of here. If I want to take all day to use my bucket, that's just what I'm gonna do."

"I don't know what your problem is, Cass. You and your dad got front page. It was a huge write-up. That was great coverage."

"You stole that picture. You promised me you wouldn't take one, and then you stole a private moment like that. You had no right. You're a jerk and a liar."

"That kind of picture melts hearts. People pay loads of money for publicity like that. And I didn't write a thing that wasn't true."

She reached down and pulled one of the balls out of the bucket then held it up menacingly at him.

"You get out of here right now, or I'll start throwing balls, all right. At you."

He shot her a nasty parting glare, but after a moment he finally took his food and walked away. His photographer followed, still snickering.

Once Cass was satisfied they wouldn't turn around and come back, she eased up off the balls and stood.

"I guess I owe you a big thanks, although I'm not used to being the one who's being rescued," Mitch said.

"You still need rescuing . . . from me." Cass took a ball and threw it at the target.

The ball smacked against it, just right of the bullseye, but it did the trick. The lever tripped, and down Mitch went with a splash.

Cass handed the bucket back to the vendor, then walked up to the tank.

Once Mitch reset the plank, he pulled himself up onto the bench.

"Woman, you are gonna pay for that one."

He reached down and splashed water at her from the tank. She squealed and ducked to the right, avoiding the largest spray, but catching a few sprinkles along the left side of her shirt, shoulder and face.

"You better be nice to me, or I'm gonna empty that whole bucket," she said and wiggled a finger at him in reprimand.

He put both hands up in surrender.

She walked closer to the tank. "Did you say your time is just about up?"

"Yeah."

"Good. The least you can do is buy me some lunch and bring it to the livestock area."

"You expect me to buy you lunch after you dunked me?"

He splashed more water at her which she tried to swat away with her hand.

She did some exaggerated eyelash batting. "Nope. I expect you to buy me lunch after I just used up all my cash saving you from our least favorite reporter."

"All right. But you have to promise to eat it with me."

"Deal." She turned in the direction of the livestock pavilion. "Now, if you'll excuse me, I have a group of future farmers to guide."

Another splash of water hit behind her as she walked away.

Later that afternoon, Cass took her place at the railing and watched the contestants line up and prepare for the market hog judging.

Sally had her cane in her left hand. The thing was almost as tall as she was. When the gate to the show ring opened, Sally touched the cane to a spot just behind the pig's ear, and it trotted into the ring.

Other contestants did the same, and their hogs chased after Sally's. All that care to line them up evaporated in an instant. They rooted around the sawdust, snorting and sniffing as they went.

Contestants weren't allowed to touch the animal on any part of the body that might be used for meat, so they could only guide their animals with pressure behind the ears and couldn't make contact with the body at all.

Despite Sally's eagerness to leave hogs behind and move onto dairy cows, she put everything she had into her show. Despite her worries that her barrow, or male, was going to be disqualified from his weight class, he'd made it into his class without any problems. That kid seriously needed to learn the word "relax."

She moved the animal into a cleanly lined stance, all the right angles to accentuate its muscles and meat.

Sally did an excellent job of splitting her focus between the judge's movements as well as on her animal and keeping him in the right position.

When she answered the judge's questions, she was all smiles and good cheer. She spoke easily to the man, and she answered quickly without having to stop and think.

Granted, judges rarely asked really tough questions. These weren't scientific inventions that had to be explained. Usually, they asked about care or feed, just enough to make sure the contestant actually understood and participated in the process of raising an animal and hadn't just left it to mom or dad to do.

When the judge moved on to the next contestant, Sally turned around to Cass and smiled. Cass recognized that expression from her own days in the ring. The hard part was over.

Two more events plus a half-hour break later, and the official called them all to order over the loudspeaker to announce the results.

After nodding off three times, Cassidy took to pacing so she could hear everything he said. She didn't want to miss hearing whether one of her kids placed. Her kids had won two blue ribbons and two reds, a decent finish. The day had finally turned around. There was one more surprise, though.

"And our last announcement of the day—be sure to offer a hearty congratulations to the pig with the most personality, the special little porker that will be the honorary grand marshal at tonight's Pig Ball, barrow number two-five-two-four, raised by Miss Sally Riley."

Sally ran up to the announcer as everyone clapped. The announcer gave her the special sash for her to wear when she paraded her into the Pig Ball. Sally's pig would also be granted a reprieve from the auction block and would be a celebrity at tonight's festivities.

Cass stepped forward before the crowd of her kids broke apart.

"Hey, you guys did a great job today. Remember that the livestock sale starts tomorrow at eight. And remember that our end-of-the-year picnic will be next weekend in the pavilion at Cumberland Springs Park."

Each of her kids offered good-byes on the way out of the show ring. Even a few parents walked up and offered a few words here and there. Stifling yawns, Cass smiled and spoke with them all.

Once the last of the families left, she checked her watch. She had an hour before the Pig Ball. She pulled out her cell phone and dialed Beth. If her friend had really meant the offer about helping her prepare, she just might make it.

Chapter Thirteen

A warm, welcoming glow shone above the pavilion inside Cumberland Springs Park. Cars and trucks lined both sides of the paved driving lanes. Bethany and Cass had been forced to park so far away from the pavilion, they could only hear a low hum of activity instead of the distinctive sounds of one of the biggest parties of the year.

"Are you sure I look okay? I've never worn so much makeup in my life," Cass said as they started the long trek toward the pavilion.

Unfortunately, their preparations had taken a little longer than the hour they started with, and they'd arrived late.

"You look like you just walked out of a movie star magazine. Stop worrying."

Beth fell into step beside Cass, and their strides created a rhythmic clip-clop against the pavement.

"Of course, I look like I just stepped off the cover," Beth said, giving her hair a sassy shake.

Bethany had chosen the shiny, sleek look for her hairdo tonight, while she'd helped Cass create large, loose curls that bounced with every step.

After several minutes of walking they were able to make out various sounds, in particular, the fiery guitar-playing and fiddle-plucking of a local bluegrass band as they cranked up "The Wabash Cannonball."

"Sounds like the Bottom of the Barrel Boys are heating it up tonight," Beth said.

"We should've worn flats instead of these heels."

"Flats aren't sexy. Heels are. It's about time *somebody* around here got you out of that 'school librarian' look."

"Falling on your butt isn't exactly sexy, either."

Her toes were already pounding, and she could just imagine the hobbling she'd be doing tomorrow as she gathered eggs.

"Then don't fall on your butt," Beth said simply.

They fell into step with a few other ballgoers, and made chitchat about favorite local topics like the weather and the fair.

Cass learned that Pop Pop's chili had been a big hit of the day, too, and he'd finally snagged the blue ribbon out from under Old Man Simpson.

Just as the discussion had turned to food, they finally

made it close enough to make out various smells from the pavilion.

The aroma of tangy barbeque drifted across their path on smoky tendrils in the air. Cass licked her lips, and her stomach growled its desire to join in the festivities.

Since the weather had cooperated, the coordinators had had the picnic tables arranged to either side of the pavilion, leaving the concrete floor space to house the dancing. The north end of the pavilion contained the stage, and the small white picket fence area reserved for king of the Pig Ball.

Glowing with pride, Sally stood beside the pen and fussed over her new porcine celebrity.

"Darn, we missed the march," Cass said. "Sally already has him in his pen."

"Oh well. At least you're not missing the main event."

Beth pointed toward the other side of the stage where Mitch stood talking with Wes Tucker and another former classmate of theirs, Skeet McIntyre.

The sight of Mitch sent goose bumps along Cass' arms. He stood a couple of inches taller than either of the other men, and he had on dark black jeans, and a crisply pressed black, button-down dress shirt.

He looked around as he listened to Wes, and when his gaze landed on Cass, he immediately straightened and smiled. He said a couple of words to the other men, then he crossed the floor and walked right up to Cass.

"I didn't know I was going to need a tux for to-night. You look gorgeous."

He leaned over and kissed her on the cheek.

Beth cleared her throat. "What am I, chopped liver?"

He reached out and tapped Beth on the arm with his fist. "Hey, Bethany. You look pretty too."

"Try not to go hoarse from lavishing all that praise."

He winked at her, then held a hand out to Cass. He locked eyes with her even though he still spoke to Bethany.

"If you don't mind, I'm going to steal your com-panion here."

"You can have her," Beth said with fake disgust. "Besides, I see both the Dyer boys, and I have some dancing to do."

Cass slipped her hand into Mitch's, and warmth flooded her body. Suddenly, it didn't matter how tired she'd been or how far she'd had to walk in ridiculously heeled shoes.

"C'mere and let me show you off on this dance floor," Mitch said into her ear as he pulled her toward the dance crowd.

She flashed him what had to be the biggest, dopi-est grin ever. She couldn't help herself. After almost coding herself into a coma this week, she finally had the chance to dance with the most handsome man in the county.

He eased his left arm around her waist and gripped her hand in his right, then they fell into a rhythm of steps and sways to match the other dancers.

She leaned in as closely as she dared and took in a deep whiff of Stetson. It had fast become her favorite smell, and she inhaled as deeply as she could.

"You look like a golden angel," Mitch said, as they moved through the crowd.

"I can't take credit for the dress. Beth picked it out. She did my shopping for me while I met with that guy in Nashville who hired me to do his Web site this week."

"The one who's puttin' you through your paces and keeping you up all night?"

She nodded. "I can't promise I'm not going to fall asleep on your shoulder during any slow dances."

"Well, I know how to wake you up."

He moved his hand from her back and held it next to her face, then snapped his fingers opened and closed against his thumb like pincers.

"Apparently someone didn't learn his lesson from getting dunked earlier today."

He smirked but quickly returned his hand to her lower back and guided her around the dance floor.

Fast or slow, they went on and on and on for at least an hour, she'd guess. Unlike some of the other couples on the floor, he never pushed her out and spun her, but held her close to him, as though he couldn't stand to let her go.

The band announced a guest female vocalist for their next number and started the slow, bittersweet strains of Pasty Cline's "Walkin' after Midnight."

She didn't know how it was possible, but Mitch pulled her even closer, and even though the difference in their heights meant she'd never be able to rest her head *on* his shoulder, she was able to nuzzle her forehead in that sweet spot between his collarbone and the side of his neck.

"I swear, Cass, it's like prom night all over again."

She looked up into his eyes, and they shared a smile at the memory. Back in those days, prom had been the most special night of her life, of both their lives, and Cass hadn't been able to imagine anything better except maybe her wedding.

Tonight was better, though.

Tonight was more than just music and food and fun. Tonight was more than a gal wearing a pretty dress, dancing with a handsome guy.

Tonight brought the realization that dreams don't have to die just because you didn't reach them the first time. Tonight meant that even though some dreams were a little harder to work for, they were that much sweeter to enjoy when you reached them.

Tonight meant that once again, she was Mitch Riley's girl, and there was no other label she could have ever wanted more.

She leaned her head against him once again and closed her eyes. She couldn't feel any knots in her shoulders from hours hunched over the keyboard. She didn't feel apprehension about her father's hearing. And worries about money didn't even register on her horizon.

Later, alone in her room, she might think about those things. Tomorrow night, after another long day of coding and a short night of sleep, she might feel those things.

For now, all the warmth, contentment, and peace she could muster flooded through her, and she held on to Mitch as tightly as she could.

A most unwelcome voice intruded on their tender moment. Ty's.

"I keep waiting for you two to take a break, so I can ask for a dance, but it's been almost half an hour."

Mitch and Cass stopped to face the intruder.

"Looks like you're going to be waiting even longer, then, doesn't it?" Mitch said.

Ty looked insistently at Cass. "There are some things I'd like to say, if you don't mind."

Cass' stomach tightened, and she clenched her jaw. Ty's words hadn't been any use to her so far, and she wasn't interested in hearing any more.

"The lady isn't interested in what you have to say."

"She hasn't heard what I have to say. C'mon, Cass, you of all people should understand the need for second chances."

He took a step closer to Cass. "Can't I have one?"

In the blink of an eye, Mitch raised his arm and put it straight out, stopping Ty from coming closer.

The couples dancing around them all stopped to stare.

"I'm going to say this one time and one time only," Mitch said in a low but forceful voice that in any other circumstance would have given Cass deliciously tingly goose bumps. "Turn around and go find something else to entertain yourself."

Ty shoved Mitch's hand away. "Or what? You'll arrest me? You think that badge gives you the right to dispense justice on your own terms?"

Mitch took a step closer to Ty. They were almost the same height, with Mitch only having an inch or two on the man. In terms of size, though, Ty didn't come anywhere near Mitch's wide shoulders and deep chest.

"The first amendment gives you the right to *say* what you want to say. It does not give you the right to try to *force* others to listen. You have something to say to her? Well, hotshot reporter, take out an ad in the paper, and *maybe* she'll read it."

Ty glanced past Mitch and gave Cass a pleading look. "Please, won't you hear me out? Don't you believe in forgive and forget or anything?"

Cass smirked. "Yeah, when the guy's actually sorry and not just saying what he thinks other people want to hear so that he can keep getting information out of them."

"What more information could I want?" Ty asked, giving an exaggerated shrug and an innocent expression—way too innocent an expression. "The article's written. My work is done. I just want to talk to you."

"I don't really care to hear *anything* else you have to say."

"C'mon, Cass, don't be like that," Ty said, and took another step closer.

"Are you deaf?" Mitch asked, putting his arm out, recreating the barrier between Ty and Cass.

Ty tried to push his way past Mitch. "I'm not afraid of you, *Deputy.*"

Before Cass could blink, Mitch punched Ty. Ty wavered on his feet then sat down hard on the floor. He gingerly touched the right side of his face.

Mitch took a step forward and towered over him.

"This isn't about being a deputy or having a badge. This is about a man whose girlfriend you're bothering."

"I'm gonna sue you. I'm going to press charges for assault and battery."

Cass stepped around Mitch. "And I'll just turn around and file charges for harassment."

Ty got up on his feet, still touching his jaw. He glared at Mitch then over at Cass then back again.

"Actually"—Mitch turned his head to face Cass—"the second Ty pushed me, he became guilty of battery against an officer, so if he *really* wants to pursue this, I'll be happy to have him escorted down to the station."

Mitch gestured to the now-thick crowd around them. "And I'm sure these witnesses here noticed who made contact first."

Nods and murmurs of support rose from the group around them.

"Book 'im, Mitch," a random male voice called from the crowd.

"Yeah!" numerous voices agreed in unison.

"Look, I'm leaving, all right?" Ty raised his hands slightly in surrender.

"I'll just make sure," Mitch said, putting a hand on the back of Ty's neck and walking him forward.

The crowd on that side immediately parted, clearing a path for Mitch to walk Ty out of there. Cass followed behind them as the group broke into a loud round of applause.

When they got to the drive, Mitch released his grip on Ty.

"I trust I'm not going to have to put you in your car and buckle the seat belt myself, am I?"

"No." Ty turned around. The clapping from the pavilion had already quieted, and the music resumed, a bouncy tune to match the air of celebration around them.

Ty narrowed his eyes as he regarded Mitch, and Cass thought she saw his lips twitch as though he were about to say more. After a moment's hesitation, however, he merely turned and walked away.

Cass moved closer to Mitch and slipped her arm through his.

"Thanks," she whispered, tilting her head to look up at Mitch.

She studied his profile and basked in the strength and security he radiated.

"My pleasure," he said, never taking his eyes off Ty's retreating figure.

The warmth in his voice, though, made her smile, and she leaned the side of her head against his upper arm and gave his bicep a squeeze.

As soon as Ty climbed into his Jeep and drove away, Mitch turned his attention to Cass.

"I hope you don't think this means I'm done showing you off on that dance floor."

"Not a chance."

Arm in arm, they made their way back to the pavilion.

Chapter Fourteen

The newspaper's headline stared back at Cassidy, practically shouting itself inside her head.

REPORTER STRUCK, SHERIFF'S DEPARTMENT COVER-UP

She didn't have to read the byline to know Ty was behind this. She gaped at the headline for a moment before she went over the article, every word. In usual sensationalistic fashion, Ty shared the story of what went down at the dance, leaving out, of course, that he started it all.

The biggest focus of his article was, as expected, Mitch's punch and how the Sheriff's Department refused to file Ty's complaints for assault or excessive force.

Cassidy looked around to see if either of her grandparents was watching her. Not seeing either of them, she folded the paper, tucked it under her arm, and headed back to her loft. She hid the newspaper in the armoire. The last things her grandparents needed was to see an article like that and be even more anxious than they already were. Already, she couldn't be sure Nana wouldn't faint going through security again.

Cass' cell phone started ringing. She grabbed it from her desk and checked the display.

"Hi, Norm. You're up early."

"Hello, Cassidy," he said, all business.

"Is something wrong? Did something happen to my dad?"

"Have you seen today's paper?"

Cass grimaced. "Actually, yeah. I was just hiding it from my grandparents. I don't want them to see it before we leave."

"That article couldn't have come at a worse time. I'm thinking about leaving Mitch out of the proceedings."

"That's a bit harsh, isn't it, Norm? That reporter had it coming, and Mitch has wonderful things to say. Besides, it's just a silly local story, isn't it?"

"If they sent it out over the wire, it might have gotten picked up, especially if it's a slow news day."

"Why would it matter?"

"If the official recognizes Mitch's name, it jeopardizes his standing as a solid witness. Your dad needs the most outstanding members of the community as witnesses for this to work."

"Mitch is still an outstanding member of the community. You're kind of making a mountain out of a mole hill."

"It's my job to worry about these things, Cassidy. That's what I do. For now, we'll still bring Mitch along."

Cass couldn't get over how plain the hearing chamber was. A single rectangular table occupied the front of the room. A pudgy, balding, ruddy-faced man in a gray suit and navy tie sat at the center of this table, facing all of them. A slender, silver recorder, smaller than a deck of playing cards, was next to him on the table, beside a thick file folder.

On the opposite side of the table sat Norm and her father. Two rows of folding chairs were behind them, and that's where Cass and the others sat.

The pudgy man opened the folder. He pressed the button on a portable recorder, cleared his throat, leaned forward and began.

"Today is the second of October, and this parole review is hereby called to order at ten o'clock in the A.M. at the Riverbend Prison in Nashville, Tennessee. This is a loss-of-life case, and I am Milton Chastain, overseeing board member, present on behalf of the Tennessee Board of Probation and Parole.

"The offender Hank French, Jr., is also present and is accompanied by counsel."

Chastain turned the page he was reading from. At that moment, the door to the chamber opened. They all turned and watched as a guard led Brother Sneed into the room.

"Witness for the offender," the guard announced while Brother Sneed waved apologetically.

Chastain pointed toward an empty seat near Pop Pop.

Cass and her grandparents sat directly behind Norm and her father. Mitch sat next to her, his arm draped around the back of her chair in a combination of protection and support.

Beside Mitch, a man and a woman sat scribbling into steno pads. Cass assumed they were members of the press. Directly behind them sat Ty and his sidekick photographer. As though Ty could sense her attention on him, he looked up at precisely that moment and winked at her.

She gritted her teeth and turned her attention back to the proceedings at the long table.

She couldn't believe how little fanfare marked the occasion. She hadn't known what to expect—a drumroll, a twenty-one-gun salute, the playing of "Taps" on a solitary bugle? There had to be *something* to mark the beginning of an event like this that could change her family's life forever, again.

Instead, all her dad got was a man clearing his throat and reading off details they all already knew.

"Mr. French, you are presently serving a sentence for involuntary manslaughter involving a vehicular homicide in which a court of law determined that you and the victim were both engaged in reckless driving, is that correct?"

Cass' father nodded.

"Could you please make your responses verbal for the purposes of the recording?"

"Yes, that's correct."

"As of today's date, you've served seven years and thirty days of your sentence. I'd like you to tell me about the events of that night."

Cass' father didn't speak for several moments. Norm offered him an encouraging pat on the back, and after many more moments, he finally spoke.

"Lots of folks wanted to blame drinkin'. They thought we were drinkin' that night, but we weren't. We went to the CSH football game that night. They just had to win one more game, and they were going to the state playoffs. We got to talkin'. It was just like when we'd been boys on the team. Guess we were feeling full of it. I don't know how to explain it. We were just messin' around, and we raced each other home." His last few words were choked with emotion, and he had to take a deep breath before he could continue. "It was an accident, a total accident. It was never supposed to happen like that."

He bowed his head, and Cass squeezed her eyes shut. When she opened them, she could see Nana dabbing at her eyes with a handkerchief.

"How do you feel about what you did to contribute to the events of that night?" Chastain asked.

"I regret it, all day, every day. It's like a movie in my head that I can't never turn off. It's the last thing I think about at night, and the thought that wakes me every morning."

Cass noticed that her dad kept his hands under the table as he spoke.

Chastain added a note to the margin of the paper on top of his stack before pulling out two more sheets of paper. He glanced over them, then set them to the side.

"Presently you work as a cook in the prison kitchen. Can you tell me about any other activities you participate in within this facility? How have you used your time in prison?"

"The kitchen's all right, but the land is my true callin'. I'd rather be out workin' the soil, but that isn't a choice we get to make. What I enjoy the most is leadin' both a *Bible* study group and a prayer group. I like doing that. We talk a lot about people in the *Bible* who made mistakes but earned forgiveness, people like Abraham, Moses, Peter, even the thieves at the crucifiction."

"Very good," Chastain said as he turned another page and skimmed it. "The board is in receipt of your residential plan. I understand you'd like to return to your family farm, is that correct?"

Her father nodded. "I'm sure my father could use the help, and I'm a . . . sixth–generation farmer. It's in my blood, and there's nothing more I'd like to return to than the farming life."

"So your employment would consist of working the farm on a full-time basis?"

"Yes, it would."

Chastain closed the folder, flipped the page on a legal pad, and began writing.

"At this time, I'd like to invite comments from the offender's counsel and/or any witnesses in support of parole for this offender."

Norm leaned closer to the microphone on his and Daddy's side of the table, and said, "My name is Norman Greer, and I serve as legal counsel for Hank French, Jr. We have prepared a collection of witnesses with statements for this parole hearing. First, I'd like to introduce Robert Sneed."

Brother Sneed stood up. Norm pointed toward the right end of the table where a single chair and microphone were. The preacher walked over and sat down.

Chastain glanced at him. "Could you please state your name and hometown, for the record. Also, state your relationship to the offender."

Cass bristled at the repeated use of "offender." What her father had done had been an isolated incident, a single event. He wasn't a habitual criminal, yet that was exactly how it sounded every time they said that word.

"I'm Robert Sneed, pastor of the First Baptist Church of Cumberland Springs, Tennessee. I'm a minister to Mr. French and the entire French family."

He turned and gestured down the row of Frenches as he spoke. When his gaze fell on Cass, he gave her an extra long nod and smile. Cass gave him a polite nod in return. She couldn't be sure what he was up to, but she didn't really care so long as it helped Daddy.

"I'll be short and sweet with what I have to say, sir. When I was first approached about coming here, I initially refused."

A brief frown creased Chastain's brow. This didn't sound like an overwhelming endorsement, so far, and Cass leaned forward. Mitch gave her shoulder a light squeeze, keeping her in her seat.

"It wasn't until I received a visit from this little lady over here"—he pointed at Cass—"that I was reminded that God's grace and forgiveness apply to *everyone* and not just those people who sit in the pew every Sunday.

"You see, there were a few of those Sunday Christians who thought our church had no place endorsing someone who'd done something like Hank here. They thought we might be lending support to people who break the law. But the fact of the matter is that they need us most. They need love and forgiveness more than anyone, and I've got a seat in the front row of my church for Hank Jr., and his lovely daughter, and their entire family. I'd be honored to have him in God's house with me every week, because he's done right while he's been in here, he did right by that daughter of his, and I know in my soul that he'll do right for our congregation and our community. Thank you."

Cass leaned back into her seat and against Mitch's arm. *Okay. Brother Bob redeemed himself with that.*

Norm leaned toward the microphone again. "Our next speaker is Deputy Mitchell Riley."

Mitch got up and walked to the witness chair. He had on a crisp, navy suit and a maroon tie. Briefly, she wondered why he hadn't opted for his uniform. Surely, Norm would have wanted him to take every chance to emphasize his role within the law enforcement community. Of course, she'd stare at him no matter what he wore. In the suit, he looked lean and powerful, a different kind of power than he wielded in his uniform. He looked sharp and smart, like he belonged in a company boardroom. Cass swooned on the inside, indulging in a secret smile as she watched Mitch settle into the chair and take his oath.

"I'm Mitchell Scott Riley, a deputy with the Cumberland County Sheriff's Department. They don't really have a word for the relationship I have with Mr. French. He was my Four-H coach. He was a leader in the community. He's a man I respect highly, both back then and even more now."

Cass couldn't be sure, but she thought her father sat up a little straighter after Mitch said that.

Mitch continued. "I've been a member of the law enforcement community for a decade now. I've seen a pretty good number of criminals. This man is no criminal. He's a good man who had something tragic happen. From the scene of the accident to the night of the arrest, throughout the trial, and even today, this man has shown nothing but remorse for the events of that night. He has served his time respectfully, and I support his parole to the fullest extent that I am able."

Mitch gave Chastain a solemn nod, then stood and returned to his place beside Cass. She would speak next, and her hands began to tremble. Norm had thought she would be the strongest out of Nana, Pop Pop and herself, but now she wished they'd chosen someone else. She wasn't ready. What if she said the wrong thing? What if Chastain thought her shaking meant she was afraid of her father? What if she did something wrong, and they denied his parole?

She could feel Mitch's moving beside her, and the warmth of his breath caressed her ear.

"You're going to do fine," he whispered.

"The next speaker is Miss Cassidy French," Norm announced.

Cass stood, and her knees threatened to buckle. She paused for a deep breath.

She was just about to step around Mitch when her

father turned and looked over his shoulder at her. When their eyes met, she saw a familiar flicker in their blue depths. It was an expression she had seen before taking the field in softball games during her youth or before walking into the ring in a Four-H competition. Hope. Encouragment. The sight of it melted her heart because for that briefest of moments, he didn't look like the sad, bitter man that life had forced him to become.

Resolve coursed through her veins. She would not let him down.

"Hi, Daddy," she mouthed at him and smiled.

She felt a firm hand grip her wrist, and she looked down to see Pop Pop's fingers wrapped around her.

"I'll tend to this, Cass," he said with such resolve in his voice and behind his eyes that she didn't dare question him.

She took her seat, and he walked over to the witness chair.

"My name is Hank French, Sr., and I'm the father of this man.

"I don't like to talk about myself much, so this shouldn't take too long. I served my country in Vietnam, and there are things I saw over there that I thought prepared me for anything else life could throw at me. But then the accident happened.

"There's no way to explain what it feels like to bury your boy. You always expect them to bury you.

"And in the beginning, I was angry at both of 'em. Angry at Junior for lettin' it happen, and angry at Rich for bein' so stupid.

"But at the end of the day, well, it don't matter how it happened or who did what or who was at fault. At the end of the day, I still walk that farm and wonder if I'm gonna have anyone to give it to."

Pop Pop looked over at Hank Jr., and Cass could almost see the lump growing in his throat. He kept looking at his son, even as he spoke.

"I guess you've probably heard your fair share of parents come in here and beg for the lives of their children, so I don't 'spect I'm gonna be much different there. But if the law says that my boy's done his time, and if the law says it's possible for him to come home, well, sir, I'd like my boy back, so I can stand there at the fence line at the end of a long, hard day, clap my son on the back, and know that life is gonna go on and that everything we do to make it go on really means somethin'."

Cass couldn't help herself, tears streamed down her cheeks. She could see Nana's shoulders shaking, so she wrapped an arm around her and hugged her from the side.

Cass looked over at Pop Pop and noticed that a single tear rolled down his left cheek, but he didn't wipe it away. He was locked in an embracing gaze with her father.

Cass noticed Mitch's hand moving in her periphery, and she could swear he wiped at his eyes before moving his hand to the bridge of his nose and pretending to scratch an itch.

She looked over at Chastain to see what, if any, effect this was having on him, but he was bent over his notepad, writing as fast as he could.

Pop Pop stood up and walked back to his seat, pausing to give his son's shoulder a squeeze as he walked by.

Chastain wrote for what felt like an eternity, but when he finally spoke Cass couldn't tell that he'd felt any emotion at all.

"At this time, I'd like to invite comments from any attendees opposed to parole for this offender or who'd like to make victim impact statements."

Cass looked around the room, but no one moved forward or indicated any interest.

"All right then," Chastain began.

Nana stood.

"I'd like to speak now," she said. "I'd like to say something on behalf of the victim."

Chastain gestured toward the microphone, and Nana made her way to it. She gripped the table as she sat down, and Cass held her breath. What in the world was Nana trying to do? And would she get through it without fainting this time?

"I'm Susan French, the mother of both Hank Jr. and Richard Allen French."

Chastain began writing on his papers again.

"I've never done anything like this before. I don't really know what I'm supposed to say. I just know that this is the part where people can talk about the victim and what all this has done to them, and, well, I couldn't stand it if this time came and went and there was nobody to talk about my son."

Nana's voice shook, but every word was clear.

Cass turned her eyes toward the ceiling, trying to will the tears not to return, but it was a lost cause. She had no idea Nana planned on doing this, and a tidal wave of emotions crashed through the room as this poor mother went on about life without her children.

"When my little Richie was born, he cried and cried until they laid him across my chest. The second he touched me, that very first moment I held him, he got quiet, and I felt this peace like I've never felt before. I always used to think to myself that Junior was my go–getter and Richie was my healer. Junior was always my strength and my energy, and Richie was always my comfort."

"After that night, I thought my world couldn't get any worse than having to lose that precious baby boy, but then things found a way to get worse. The state took away my rock, and I've had to mourn them both every moment ever since.

"You call this the victim impact phase, and I'll tell you the impact on me and my family. There's a hole in my heart that's never gonna get filled back up. But there's a hole at my table that could get filled back up, with the presence of the one son I still have.

"We never asked for Junior to be excused for what happened. But if we have the chance to be as whole of a family as we're ever gonna be again, then I have to say that that's the only thing that's going to help me deal with the impact of all that's happened to our family."

Cass had to push the backs of her hands against her cheeks like windshield wipers to keep up with the tears pouring down her face. She looked up at Mitch, and he didn't even try to pretend he wasn't crying this time.

She reached up and wiped away his tears. After a moment, they wrapped their arms around one another.

Cass couldn't say how long they were like that, but when they finally parted, and she looked over to Pop Pop, he was on his feet holding Nana.

Cass turned her attention to her dad who was hunched over the table, his shoulders shaking with silent sobs.

She glanced at Chastain, who was bent even deeper over his notes, but she managed to see what looked like a tear track glistening on his right cheek.

She checked over her shoulder to where Ty was sitting. He didn't look affected at all, but merely sat writing notes as though all Nana had done was recite a grocery list.

Chastain cleared his throat. "I'd like to continue, if we could."

Pop Pop guided Nana to her seat, and everyone turned their attention forward where Chastain made a couple of additional notes, then closed the folder.

"My recommendation is in favor of parole for this offender, and I'll be forwarding that recommendation—along with the transcript of these proceedings—to the remainder of the board. This parole hearing is now concluded."

He reached over and turned off the recorder.

Cass blinked once but kept staring straight ahead. Did he really say what she thought he said? He was going to *recommend* parole?

She and Nana and Pop Pop and Mitch all stood up and hugged.

They were still hugging when a male voice called sharply from behind them, "We're ready to escort you folks out now. There's going to be another hearing in a few minutes."

They broke apart to celebrate with Norm and Hank Jr., but both men were gone.

"Where's my father?" Cass asked the corrections officer.

"He's being returned to his cell."

Cass frowned. "Can't we say good-bye?"

The officer shook his head. "This isn't a visitation day. Sorry."

Nana and Cass both sighed at the exact same moment.

The group made the trip back to the parking lot. Cass noticed the familiar outline of Brother Sneed ahead of them, and she scurried to catch up to him.

"Brother Bob," she called. He turned around. "I wanted to thank you for making the trip down here and saying what you did."

The corners of his mouth curled into a warm smile.

"As soon as you left my office, I knew what needed to be done. Peace and love be with you."

"You, too," she said, waving.

As she walked back to her family, she noticed Ty approaching from the other side. He was pulling a camera out of his bag. She ran at him.

"You have enough for the story. You're not getting anymore," she said, pointing at his camera.

He turned on the camera, and she shook her head.

"I just wanted to see if you or your grandparents wanted to make a statement. This thing takes up to two minutes of video, in addition to pictures."

"I said, no," Cass said insistently.

Mitch's voice was behind her. "Is there a problem?"

Cass glanced at Mitch. He squared his shoulders and leaned just the slightest bit forward, almost as though he *hoped* there'd be a problem. She looked back to Ty.

Ty shook his head. "There's no problem."

"Maybe I have a problem, then," Mitch said in a voice with such a low and lethal tone to it, it gave Cass goose bumps. "Maybe I have a problem with reporters who don't get their facts straight before they go to print on a story. I don't take kindly to people who smear the truth so badly, they get other people suspended for doing nothing more than trying to keep the peace."

Cass blinked. Mitch had been suspended? That was why he wasn't in uniform for the hearing?

"They suspended you?" Ty asked, and a triumphant grin spread across his face.

"Three days, pending the results of an investigation," Mitch said, then smirked. "And all of us standing here know as soon as they talk to the witnesses what the outcome will be." Mitch took a step closer to Ty. "And if I were you, Mr. Thomas, I wouldn't so much as run a stop sign anywhere in this county."

Ty pointed at him. "See what I mean. It's a conspiracy!"

Cass rolled her eyes. "I got this."

"Believe me, he is *all* yours," Mitch said. "But let me know if you need a hand. I'll be more than happy to repeat the scene from the Pig Ball."

Cass turned back to Ty.

"I was thinking about what you said about second chances," Cass began.

"Are you going to give me one?"

"What makes you think you deserve one? Just because you *want* one?"

Ty gave her a charm-filled shrug and smile. "Well, yeah."

Cass shook her head. "That's not the way it works."

"How does it work, then? What's it take?"

Cass looked around the parking lot and chose her words carefully. "It would take being a totally different person. It would take being something you're not."

His eyes registered no recognition, no understanding of what she meant.

"Some people look at a situation and see the good that's there. Some people look at a situation and see the bad that's there. You look at a situation, and what you seem to see is the best way to turn it into something scandalous, something that you can weave with intrigue so you can shock everyone."

"That's not true Cass. You're caught up in this very emotionally charged situation. You're living with something most people will never have to live with, but that they want to know about because they can't imagine what this situation must be like. You think it's boring and uninteresting only because it's *your* everyday life."

It was Cass' turn to shrug. "Whether that's true or not, I don't know. I don't care. But I can see with my own eyes that you're missing something. I watched you in there, when Nana was talking. There wasn't a dry eye in the place. Even the judge was moved by what she had to say. But when I looked at you, all you could do was stare and take notes and figure out what kind of way to spin it for your article. Just like the way you turned what happened at the Pig Ball with Mitch. You get some sick pleasure out of manipulating a situation so you control how people feel, how they think.

"The truth is, Ty, it wouldn't matter how many chances I gave you. You just don't have what it takes to empathize with people. You only have what it takes to entertain them. You don't need to be here in Cumberland Springs. You need to be in New York or LA, somewhere where people crave sensationalism, not somewhere where people crave normalcy."

"What makes you think *this* is normal?"

"What makes you think it's not? What makes you want to pick my family apart and point out everything that's wrong? Why didn't you write a story about how strong we are? About how we endure, even in the face of all this difficulty?"

Ty paused, and Cass could almost hear the gears turning in his head.

"That's a great idea."

Cass just shook her head, then she put her hands on her hips and glared at him. "What did you want to talk to me about so badly the night of the Pig Ball?"

He straightened and looked at her questioningly, but recognition dawned on his face. "Oh, that."

"Yeah, that."

He made another shrug that, had she not known

better, she might have mistaken for shyness. "You looked so pretty that night. I just wanted to dance with a pretty girl."

Cass smirked. "Cut the crap. If all you wanted was to dance with a pretty girl, you could have asked Beth or half a dozen other gals who were there that night."

"You don't get it, Cass. I wanted to dance with *this* pretty girl," he said, gesturing toward her for emphasis.

She shook her head.

"Why do you find it so hard to believe that I genuinely like you, Cass? If you'd get over that cop knockoff, and give me a chance, I could show you that I'm really a nice guy. And I really do like you."

She took a step closer to him and looked straight into his eyes.

"Actually, I *do* find it pretty easy to believe you *like* me. But like is all you'll ever be capable of. I saw you in there. When Nana talked, all you could do was work that news angle. She was pouring her heart out, and you couldn't stop to soak it in.

"Yeah, you might *like* me, but you could never *love* me. You will only ever love two things: the chase of the story, and hearing yourself talk."

For the first time in the entire time she had known Ty, not only was he at a complete loss for words, but there was, at long last, a single genuine expression on his face: Shock.

She turned and walked back to Mitch and her grandparents. Mitch slipped an arm around her shoulders.

"You gonna be all right?" he asked.

"I'll be fine," she said, squeezing him in a tight, side hug. "Why didn't you tell me about the suspension?"

"I figured the grapevine had already done it for me. Besides, it's with pay, and it won't be a big deal. Just don't be surprised when a deputy comes to see you who isn't me."

"Oh, all right, but you're the only deputy I *want* to see."

Mitch kissed her right temple. "You can say that again."

"And you can do that again," she said, leaning against his lips.

He chuckled and indulged her, all the way back to the farm.

Even though Cass hated to see Mitch go, she let out a definitive sigh of relief when both Mitch's and Norm's tail lights disappeared down the driveway and back toward town. The events and stresses of the day had worn them all out, and the last thing Nana needed to do after that was to have to come home and have to work on a big meal. Cass set out a plate of cold cuts, bread, and fixings for everyone to build their own sandwiches.

"I was thinking," Nana said as they all sat down to the table.

"Uh oh," Pop Pop said then winked at Cass.

Nana swatted at Pop Pop with her napkin. "I was thinking that we could clear out the back bedroom of all the old junk in there, then we could fix it up for Junior, so he could make it his own when he comes home."

The back bedroom had been an add-on to the house that Nana and Pop Pop had used for each of their parents when they had no longer been able to live on their own.

"I think that's a great idea, Nana," Cass said, brightening at the thought of something to help them pass the time before the parole board rendered its official decision.

Pop Pop bit into his sandwich and chewed slowly.

"What's wrong with that idea?" Nana asked him.

"I know how you are. Don't go gettin' your hopes up. Norm said they have thirty days, and a lot could happen between now and then. If you do all that work, then he doesn't get out—"

Pop Pop didn't finish the thought, at least not out loud. He took another bite.

"That's just silly, Hank. They're going to let him out. Norm said he's done everything that he can to earn it."

Pop Pop fixed a hard stare on Nana. "We both know that life isn't always fair, Susan."

Cass felt like the temperature had just dropped about twenty degrees in the room.

Nana didn't fight. She just shrugged. "I don't see the harm in being prepared. Sooner or later, he *will* be home."

"Suit yourself. I'm gonna change clothes and go work in the barn," Pop Pop said.

He took his plate to the counter, wrapped his sandwich in a paper towel, then pulled a can of Coke from the fridge before moving toward the bedrooms.

"I'll help you," Cass said as soon as Pop Pop left. "I think it's a great idea."

"Thank you, dear," Nana said with a grateful smile.

"Susan, you better come in here," Pop Pop called from the bedroom. "The answering machine is going haywire. All the lights are blinking, and the number thing says thirty-two."

Nana gaped at Cass. "Thirty-two messages? We've never had more than four before!"

They hurriedly joined Pop Pop.

"Go ahead and press 'play,' Hank," Nana said.

"I'm not touching that fool contraption," Pop Pop replied.

Nana reached over with an exaggerated sigh and hit the button.

"Susan, this is Frances Dudley. Did you see today's paper? We've got to do something about that horrible reporter. Call me."

Cass groaned and put her face in her hands. Ty's stupid article about Mitch. The town had seen it and reacted while they had all been at her father's hearing. No wonder there were thirty-two messages.

The machine beeped at the end of the first message, then another began.

"Susan, it's Immelda Watts. I've got half a mind to march into that newspaper office and let them have a good, old-fashioned tongue-lashing—"

"She's only got half a mind, period," Pop Pop said.

Cass cracked a smile, but Nana swatted at him.

A heavy sigh soon replaced Cass' grin. She was going to have to go get the paper and let them in on the story.

"I know that guilty look," Nana said. "Cass, what do you know about this?"

"I might as well show you the newspaper. Ty wrote up a nasty article about the fight at the Pig Ball, trying to make it sound like he didn't do anything wrong, like Mitch beat him up for no reason at all. Then he accused the sheriff's department of closing ranks to protect their own 'cause no one would help him file a complaint." She clenched her jaw and added sourly, "Not that it mattered. Mitch got suspended anyways."

"Suspended?" Pop Pop rolled his eyes. "See what all that political correctness gobbledygook gets ya'?"

Nana's eyes narrowed, and her lips tightened into a thin, pink line. "You knew that, and you didn't tell us?"

Cass did her best to be firm but not rebellious. "Today was going to be hard enough. There was no need to add more grief. And I didn't know about Mitch's suspension until after the hearing, when Ty came up to us."

"That boy needs a hickory switch 'cross his backside," Pop Pop said as he went to the closet and pulled out a faded pair of overalls.

"I couldn't agree more," Nana said as she opened the small drawer of the nightstand. She removed a yellow address book with a large sunflower on the cover. Dozens of scraps of paper stuck out of it at all kinds of angles, the footnotes of three generations of Cumberland Springs residents. "Now, if you'll excuse me, I have a few phone calls to make. I'll be in the office."

Nana walked out.

Pop Pop unknotted his tie. "I hope that boy says his prayers tonight. 'Cause tomorrow he's gonna step into World War Three."

Cass crossed the room to him and kissed his cheek. "I'm going to tidy up the kitchen, then see what Web work I need to do. G'night, Pop Pop."

"Now, wait just a second. There's somethin' in your hair there, somethin' shiny, why—"

He reached up and pulled his hand back with a bright silver quarter in his grip.

Cass smiled and took it.

Pop Pop made a low whistle. "Remind me to come to you when I need my next loan on the farm."

She winked at him. "You got it."

As she made her way to the kitchen, though, worry tugged at her heart. She hated to hear Pop Pop talk about needing money. She hurriedly cleaned up their dinner, grabbed a can of Mountain Dew, and headed off to her computer and the only thing she knew to do about it.

The next morning, when Cass brought the eggs in, she smelled no bacon when she walked into the kitchen. Champ wasn't by the door, and when she glanced at the stove, it was empty of any skillets or pans. Instead, on the counter sat six bowls, each one with a packet of instant oatmeal in it and an apple beside it.

Cass' face and stomach twitched at the same time. Instant oatmeal? Blech!

Cass went to the sink and washed her hands. She wouldn't even pretend she could whip up a meal on par with Nana's, but she could at least fry up some bacon and egg sandwiches.

She looked at the bowls again. Six couldn't be right. One for her, Nana, Pop Pop, the two Dyer boys . . . who could the last one be for? She shrugged and went to the refrigerator. When she opened the door, she paused. Inside were big bowls filled with egg salad mix, enough for lunch sandwiches for about half a dozen people. Whatever Nana had planned to unleash on Ty, she didn't plan on being around to cook today, but she did plan on an extra guest.

"Poor thing must've been up all night," Cass said to herself as she located the eggs and bacon and pulled them from the fridge.

The back door opened, and Cass could hear the wiping of boots on the mat.

"Mornin', Pop Pop. Don't pay any attention to that oatmeal on the counter. I'll make some bacon and egg sandwiches since Nana's tied up. What time did she finally come to bed last night?"

"I wouldn't have that information, ma'am," Mitch said from the doorway.

Cass spun around and took in the sight of Mitchell Scott Riley in overalls and a red-and-black checkered flannel shirt, rolled up past his elbows. He had a John Deere cap on his head and a tall thermos in his left hand, and Cass put out a steadying hand on the counter before her knees buckled.

"Hey," she said, flashing him a big, dopey grin. "What're you doing here?"

"Suspension, remember?" Putting the thermos on the counter, he added, "I told your grandfather yesterday that I had some extra time on my hands if he needed any help."

"But, what about your dad? Wouldn't he rather have you helpin' out there?"

Mitch shrugged and walked over to her.

"I like the view better over here," he said, then he leaned down and kissed her.

His lips were warm and tender, and he smelled like the field, all earthy and organic. Cass' heart began dancing a jig in her chest, and prickles of delight skipped from head to toe, just beneath her skin.

After a few moments, their lips parted, although neither of them moved.

"So, good morning," Mitch said, and his breath danced over her lips.

She smiled and lost herself in those gorgeous green eyes.

"Unfortunately, I can't stay long," he said and took a step back. "I just came for more coffee. I'll tell the boys you're making a hot breakfast."

"Come back in half an hour, and it'll be ready," she said, studying him as he filled the thermos.

She didn't know which Mitch she liked best; the man in uniform, the man on the stand, or the man of the field. Not that she really had to choose one, she supposed. They were all him, and, if luck was on her side this time, they would all be hers.

Joy pooled in her stomach and radiated out to every part of her. Dark, dreary days of waiting for her father had hung over her like a storm cloud, and now, Mitch shone down on her like the sun. Now that she actually had some sunshine, she couldn't imagine what to do with it. Overwhelmed, she closed her eyes and tightened her grip on the counter. Her knees very well *could* buckle at any moment.

"Man, I haven't worked like this in ages," Mitch said, snapping her out of her reverie. "I bet I'm stiff and sore for the next couple of days."

She opened her eyes and watched as he took several deep shoulder shrugs, testing himself.

"There's a rub that Nana puts on Pop Pop's back. I'm sure I could snag some for you before you leave." She lowered her voice. "If you say 'pretty please,' I bet I could put it on for you too."

Mitch flashed her that dimpled smile that made her go even more queasy on the inside.

"Tempting as that sounds, I actually have a better idea. How about a midnight trip to the springs?"

"You can't patrol out there if you're suspended, can you?"

Mitch put one hand on his left hip then scratched his chin, looking skyward. "Hmm, I can't remember. Did he ask me to check in on that as a deputy or a friend? I just can't remember."

Cass grinned. "All right. I'm game."

He picked up the thermos. "I'll need to soak these old bones, so bring your suit this time."

Cass shook her head. "I don't wanna mess with a swimsuit."

Mitch shrugged and flashed a wry grin. "Fine by me. Don't bring it. Either way, you're going in."

Cass pulled the dishtowel from the door handle of the refrigerator and swatted at him. "All right, back to work!"

He scooted out the door, chuckling as he pulled it closed behind him.

There was good news and bad news aplenty the next day. Mitch's suspension lasted only twenty-four hours, so they got just their one extra night at Cumberland Springs, then he had to be back at work.

Not only did the usual smells of a hearty breakfast greet Cass when she came into the kitchen, the cheerful sound of Nana's humming greeted her, as well. Cass put away the basket of eggs, then walked in to find the newspaper occupying the center of the table. Cass' lips curled into a certifiable ear-to-ear grin as she read the headline:

REPORTER DISMISSED AMID CONTROVERSY, COMPLAINTS

"Nana, is this what you were up to yesterday?"

"Never underestimate the power of a ticked off quilting circle."

Cass read the article. After a "group of concerned citizens" flooded the newspaper phones with calls, then staged a sit-in of the offices themselves, Ty Thomas was dismissed from the staff of the *Cumberland Press*. A note at the end of the article also announced that the *Cumberland Press* was currently taking applications for a new receptionist since there had been a sudden departure after yesterday's events.

"Way to go, Nana! That's *my* grandma."

"Guess the old girl's still got it when she needs it."

"Remind me never to cross you."

"That's one thing you'll never have to worry about, Cassidy, for all the rest of our days."

Cass kept up with her Web work and with helping Nana on her fixer-upper project. Every night after supper, Pop Pop would disappear out to the barn while Nana and Cass worked on the mother-in-law room. In a week's time, they had it spic and span and ready for its resident.

Nana had just started thinking out loud about whether or not she had enough time to make a new quilt for the old, oak four-post bed when Pop Pop appeared in the doorway.

"Before you do all that, I have another project for you. Find a place for this."

He backed away from the door, then he reappeared with a rocking chair. He carried it over and set it a few feet away from the bed.

Nana put her hands up to her face as she looked over the newly finished rocker.

Cass could smell the fresh varnish on the chair from across the room.

Pop Pop stepped back, took a red bandanna from the right pocket of his overalls and wiped his forehead.

"Is this what you've been doing out there all week, Hank?"

"You're right, Susan," he said in what sounded like

an apologetic voice. "Sooner or later, our boy's gonna be home. And he's gonna need somewhere to sit when he reads or watches the game or whatever he wants to do with his time."

Nana walked over and hugged him, then she gave him a kiss that almost made Cass blush.

She quietly stepped into the hall, giving them their privacy. Now, all that was left to do was to find out if Daddy would be home sooner, or if it would be later.

Chapter Fifteen

Almost four weeks had passed since Cass' father's hearing, and she did everything she could to bring good luck her family's way.

She went to church every week and prayed. She ate all her vegetables. And she took on all the Web site jobs she could handle but still keep up her farm chores, as well.

Granted, none of the assignments brought in as much money as the Echo Enterprises one had, but none of them left her bleary-eyed or pushed her past the brink of exhaustion, either.

She split the money evenly between herself and her grandparents, although she didn't let them know that. They never would have taken a check from her;

instead, she set up a special account at Whitley Trust Bank and arranged for the farm's mortgage payment to come from it.

Whitley himself came to the farm to deliver the news that the Frenches had a mysterious benefactor, but Nana and Pop Pop figured out who it was. After Whitley left, they both hugged her like they'd never hugged her before. Nana cried, and even Pop Pop teared up.

Cass made sure to leave plenty of time for Mitch too. They made a habit of playing security patrol to the Cumberland Springs every Friday night now that things were all official again. And because the price of gas was so ridiculous, they also perfected the art of the long walk with all the talking, tickling, and flirting it entailed.

So when Mitch asked her to take a drive, she was a little surprised, but she accepted immediately. She scooted next to him on the seat, and he curled his right arm around her shoulders while they rolled down the driveway.

A swell of pride filled her as they drove away from her grandparents' farm, and she could see it, captured like a photograph, in the side mirror.

The sight of it had always given her a smile, but now that she actually contributed toward its success in a more substantial way, she felt more than simple relief seeing the old family homestead.

They had barely driven a mile from the farm when Mitch pulled into a driveway and stopped in front of a locked gate.

"Another security patrol?" Cass asked as she watched Mitch unbuckle his seat belt.

"Not this time," he said, then climbed down from the truck, took a key from his pocket, and unlocked the padlock and chain on the gate.

He climbed back into the truck, but he didn't put it in gear right away. He turned to her, and there was a seriousness etched on his face that made her stomach lurch.

"Three years ago, this property came up for sale. It was twenty acres, but I couldn't afford that, so I talked the bank into letting me buy the front five, as long as I agreed to put in a driveway to the back if anyone else bought it. And you know the economy around here. No one's buying land. Secretly, I keep hoping I can get promoted and get the funds together to buy up the rest, or qualify for a loan for it."

Cass turned and looked at the property. It was gorgeous land, dotted with walnut and pine, and all sorts of other trees. The front third had recently been cleared of the brush and weeds, but the back was choked with them. It'd take a lot of work to whip this place into shape.

"The soil has too much shale in it to be good farmland, but it'd be a great place to have horses or livestock. Mostly, I really just want to build a house here. At first I wanted it because, well . . ."

Cass looked at him. His left hand gripped the steering wheel so hard that his knuckles had whitened.

"Go ahead," she said, offering an encouraging smile as she looked into his eyes once more.

"I thought it was the closest I was ever going to get to you again. I knew you were living on your grandparents' farm and that it'd probably be yours some day, and so I wanted to be as close as I could in case I ever heard your address come over the scanner. I wanted to be there if you ever needed help."

A lump of emotion welled up in her throat.

He kept going. "I never dreamed I'd get another chance like this, Cassidy. And now, instead of listening to the scanner and waiting to be called in from the sidelines, I want to be part of the action. I want to build a home here, with you."

He reached over and opened the glove box, pulling a small, black velvet box from inside. He opened the box and inside was a beautifully dainty gold ring with three round diamonds on it: the largest one in the center, and two smaller ones to either side.

How her heart didn't explode in her chest right then and there would forever remain a mystery.

"So will you take another walk with me . . . down the aisle?" Mitch asked, and she could have sworn she heard his voice crack on the last word.

"You better believe it," Cass said and stuck out her left hand.

Mitch fumbled getting the ring out of the box, but he slipped it on her finger at last.

"There's just one thing," Cass said, looking down and wiggling the fingers of her left hand as she admired the new decoration. She loved it and wiggled them again and again.

"What's that?" he asked, a definite strain of worry in his voice.

"Can we wait until after my father's out? I mean, in case he doesn't get parole this time. I want him to walk me down the aisle."

He let out a half-laugh. "You got it."

Then he leaned in and kissed her, and she pressed her lips to his with all the eagerness, joy, and love she had to give him. She kissed him like a woman who had just won love's lottery.

Epilogue

Cass had to hand it to her grandmother. When she made up her mind she wanted something done, it got donc.

So when Nana put her mind to making sure her son had the biggest Thanksgiving feast ever for his first holiday home, then a feast is exactly what they had, even though it meant she and Cass had to get up before that persnickety old rooster to hit the kitchen at four in the morning to cook both a turkey *and* a ham.

Every day afterward father and son rose from the breakfast table and went to work the fields together. By Christmas, not only had Hank Jr.'s cough disappeared, but he had color and muscle that had evaporated from him in prison.

Of course, all that was a distant memory by the spring thaw. On that first day of spring, Cassidy Anne French walked down the aisle of the First Baptist Church on her father's arm. With her best friend Beth to her left, she stood before Brother Sneed and married Mitchell Scott Riley, the man who had stepped on her toes all those years ago in Selby's Diner and stolen her heart forever.